Enigmatic Tales

Larry Lefkowitz

Fomite
Burlington, VT

ISBN-978-1-947917-09-5
Library of Congress Control Number: 2019933768
Fomite
58 Peru Street
Burlington, VT 05401
www.fomitepress.com

for
my wife
my children
my grandchildren

Contents

Gershon's Bus Ride

Gershon is sitting on the bus with two baskets brim full of purchases from the open-air market at his feet, one basket crowding his legs, the other half in the aisle, a traditional arrangement on Jerusalem's buses as they aren't designed for ample purchases. Jerusalemites like to purchase in bulk. They have large families. Besides, at any time someone or many someones may "drop in." Gershon's wife, Rachela, who was not blessed with children, likes people to drop in. She is fond of quoting Gershon who quotes from the Mishna: 'Let your house be open wide.'

As he usually does, Gershon looks out the window. He likes to watch the people, his fellow Jerusalemites, his people – or part of them, the ones dressed in black, or at least modestly. It is the Hebrew month of Elul, the gate to atonement, to forgiveness, for which modesty is especially appropriate.

If this was the extent of Gershon's interest – looking out the window – we wouldn't have much of a story. But then his ear picks up the conversation of two men sitting behind him. "Conversation" is not the best word. It isn't a conversation about family, or apartments, or business. It is about the Torah. Gershon strains to hear the discussion, the dispute, the pilpul in adherence to the commandment to occupy oneself with the study of Torah.   The discussion includes opinions taken from the whole course of Jewish history: to employ the Hebrew image, a 'wide tent-cloth', indeed.

He leans back in his seat to hear better whenever the driver puts on the brakes, or passes a truck, or street noises make it difficult to hear. Each word can be important. Is it not written: 'One who learns from his friend one chapter, or one paragraph, or even one letter, must be given honor'?

Gershon does not turn his head in order to look at the two men. First of all, it might give them the feeling that their conversation disturbs him, though nothing could be further from the truth. Second, they might pause and lose the thread of their thoughts and all three of them would lose.

The discussion increasingly fascinates Gershon. So much so that he misses his stop and doesn't realize it until three stops later. It doesn't matter, Gershon is caught as any worthy Jew would be. Although he continues to look out the window, he sees nothing; his whole being is focused on the debate, according to the Hebrew idiom, "all of him an ear".

The two men get up and pass him, still talking. One makes his points quietly, the other gesticulates for emphasis. Gershon, a closed man, feels sympathy for the quieter of the two. But this is a superficial aspect and, of course, does not affect his sympathies with regard to the positions taken. This is a debate about Torah, not a popularity contest. He gets quickly to his feet and follows them, completely forgetting his baskets.

He thrusts his foot in the bus door closing behind them so that it reopens, and succeeds in slipping out, descending after the two disputants without losing the thread of their discussion. He follows them, hoping that they will resolve the dispute, or at least agree to disagree, but only after each has amassed his points. In such discussions the conclusion (if one is reached) is secondary to all that has gone before. He walks silently after them, not only to hear, but also to not be discovered. Although he is cumbersome in build, he is light on his feet, and so does not fall behind. Has not Rashi explained: 'The Holy One, blessed Be He, makes the righteous wait and only reveals things to them afterwards'?

Why is it so important to Gershon to know why if you find a mother bird sitting with chicks or eggs in a nest, you must send her away before taking the chicks or eggs? What a question! He's a Jerusalemite. He lives in the Holy City. He – where were we? The matter is far more than a question of being merciful to the mother bird. The discussion has gone long and far beyond that point, branching out and focusing on other points and further conundrums, and as it branched out, Gershon felt he did so with it. Each disputant called upon the rabbis and sages to bolster his position: The Rambam, Abarbanel, Ibn-Ezra, the Gaon from Vilna. Gershon listens wide-eared at their erudition.

After a time, the two men sit on a bench, apparently not in any hurry, and continue their deliberations. For a second Gershon panics. He can hardly sit next to them; they might remember him from the bus and become suspicious, or they might cease their discussion altogether. Blessed be He, there is a tree nearby. The creation lacks for nothing. As it is written in the Ethics of Our Fathers: 'How pleasant this tree!'

Gershon is relieved to see there is no nest with a bird with chicks or eggs in the tree; first of all, because his girth would be an impediment to his climbing the tree and performing the mitzvah and, second, he would lose the thread of the discussion. At first Gershon hides behind the tree, but the two men, deep in dispute, are oblivious to his presence. As it is said: "If two sit together and there are not words of the Torah spoken between them, then this is a session of sinners." Gershon leans against the tree and listens. It is the month of Elul, crisp and tangy as an apple yet at the same time autumnally sad, uplifting yet weighty. A rare peacefulness suffuses Gershon, who feels a one-ness with the world.

Minutes pass. More than minutes pass. It is as if the world has ceased to turn for a second time. But the world is only one of many worlds in the Lord's firma-ment, while the Torah is the world of worlds. Finally, the discussion comes to an end. All points have been covered. Have the issues been resolved? That is not the point. In the end the Creator resolves. Man tries to understand.

The two disputants shake hands and go their separate ways. Gershon wants to run after one, after both, to shake their hands. To express his gratitude. He doesn't do it lest they discover he was listening; moreover, they might think him a bit crazy. His wife Rachela sometimes tells him he is crazy, but she does so more in praise than condemnation. There is also the technical problem of how to manage to shake both their hands as the distance between the two widens.

Tears in his eyes, uplifted as only a real Jew can be by a brilliant Talmudic discussion, he returns home, "light-footed as a deer." To his surprise the sky is beginning to darken. So much time has passed? For the first time he remembers that his wife had expected him home much earlier with two full baskets for the Sabbath. Yachin and Boaz, he calls the baskets to Rachela's delight, in honor of the two wide-girthed pillars which supported the Holy Temple in Jerusalem, may it be rebuilt speedily in our day, amen. Sometimes the baskets cause Gershon to think of the first fruits brought to Jerusalem on the Feasts of the Pilgrimage. And if in those days someone mislaid the first fruits before reaching the Temple, the way he himself just forgot the baskets on the bus, was there some remedy for this – perhaps a certain sacrifice? No time now to dwell on this; Rachela will have already lit the candles.

When he tells Rachela why he is late, she will understand. It is the month of Elul. What are two baskets on the scales against seeking eternal truths?

Apparently, Gerson's 'disappearance' is not the first, and for the same reason. He tries to remember if in the past there were also occasions when he forgot the baskets. Rachela stands, hands on hips. "I see once again you became immersed in a discussion of Torah on the bus?"

Although she says this as a question, she realizes it is in actuality a fact.

Gershon reddens. "Yes, Rachela, I didn't mean to, but . . ."

She saves him from groping for an explanation. "It's ok, Gershon," she smiles at him. "I have a husband who is, in his way, a Torah scholar."

"Yes, as it is written: "If not now, when?"

Rachela nods, "You come back from your 'studies' full of wise sayings."

Gershon beamed at her. "Of which one of the wisest is, 'find a wife, find a good thing.'"

Miriam's Song

Until our tenth birthday, my sister and I were one person, fraternal twins, our closeness was not hindered, but enhanced, by our difference in gender. Our thoughts were as one thought. Since we could feel what the other was thinking, we had no need to speak. It was not until our third birthday that we spoke our first words, and then at the same time according to our mother, "Only because you had to communicate with the outside world," by which she meant the rest of the family. When reminded by the shtetl women about our slowness in speaking – for signs of intelligence were eagerly sought in shtetl children and speaking early was one of them – she would reply, "Why should they speak? They speak to each other without speech. Even after they learned to speak, they talked with their father and me less than other children talk with their parents." It was clear that she felt apart, especially from her daughter whom it was her duty to train in the ways of the home. As for me, Miriam, my sister, my twin, was more a mother to me.

We preferred our own company to that of other children. On the infrequent occasions when we joined their games, we had the advantage. In hide-and-seek we knew where the other was hiding and would mentally warn of whoever was "it". And when one of us was "it", we never "found" the other person – that was a rule unspoken, like all our rules. The game, like everything we did, was our conspiracy against the rest of the world, against our parents, against everything that was not us.

We were the darlings and the mystery of the shtetl. Adam and Eve we were called, since we seemed each a part of the other.

While I learned Torah, Miriam, as a girl groomed for the home, was taught only a few prayers, yet, to the astonishment of everyone but us, she knew as much as I did. Whatever I learned she absorbed simultaneously. When I was honored with a ceremony on completion of my studies, I felt she felt she had earned it, too. The residents of the shtetl began to call us "Double

Ayin" for the Hebrew verbs where the two same letters coming together are written as one letter. "Hello, Double Ayin," they would say, whether addressing me, or Miriam, or us together.

Our most amazing feat in the eyes of the shtetl was our ability to suddenly start singing the same song at the same time without previous signal, even if we started in the middle, as we sometimes did. In this we were like the shofars of Reb Zalman and Reb Elya: if one was blown, the other would reverberate.

Our closeness continued, two magnets in each other's pull, until our tenth birthday when, as on every one that had gone before, we received gifts we considered ours rather than mine. But then, at 10 o'clock in the morning – so vividly is it fixed in my memory – it happened.

We were sitting in the kitchen, nibbling on the after-breakfast snacks left by mother to tide us over from breakfast to lunch, when my twin began singing a song I had never heard, a song without words. Although I had never heard the melody before, it was not the melody that turned my blood to ice. She was singing alone, and not because I chose not to join in: I hadn't felt the song. I could only stare at her, numbed into a speechlessness that was the first born of our failure to communicate, and if she was aware of my surprise (as I have no doubt that she was), she showed no sign. From that moment, we were two people instead of one.

Each day our separation increased, gradual though it was. It did not involve hostility, it was simply her refusal to share – an absence, rather than a conflict – a withholding of herself that grew. In the beginning, I implored her with my thoughts, "What has happened? Why?" but she closed off her mind to me. It was as if she had died, and yet she had not died, or rather, her soul had died and her body had lived. "What happened to the Double Ayin?" people asked. "They are growing up," mother answered. "One's a boy and the other's a girl, they have different interests." She believed this explanation, and so did everyone else. People began to call us by our separate names.

Miriam would sing none of the old songs, only that wordless song which was the first she refused to share, walking to it in the slow steps of a pavan; and if I were present, to her it was as if I was not there.

Except for the song, she became silent – not only to me, which had always been so, we never needed words – but to others. Her behavior was so noticeably different that the shtetl began to contrast her conduct to mine, treating us as different instead of the same -- to the praise of me and the criticism of her. But I felt no glow in their praise . . . I had now become one of them, and Miriam was alone. What made me despair was her refusal to be aware of my solitude. For her to have known how I felt and yet refuse reconciliation would have been painful, but that she refused to know how I felt left me struggling to hold on to my sanity.

In addition to her silence, Miriam began to sleep during the day, to the distraction of a mother whose imploring concerns were met with silence, as if she had not heard her questions. At night Miriam would walk through the house, sometimes silent, sometimes singing the song, which by now was called "Miriam's song."

I would watch her in her sleep-like walk, as devoted to her as she was oblivious to my presence. When I placed myself in her path, she walked around me in her slow, dignified pavan, as if I were a chair which had been moved from its accustomed place. I was tempted to grab her, to stop her, to clamp my hand over her mouth to end the song – futile as this would have been since it seemed to emanate from her even when she was silent, as though the song had replaced that part of her that once was me. But I never did.

Something restrained me, perhaps the fear of losing her for good, or of her turning on me physically – something she had never done – and which I could not live with.

If Miriam was not already the object of whispers, the conduct of which I am now to speak, made her so. She would leave the house at night to walk within the shtetl singing her song as she used to walk within the house, as though she refused any longer to be confined by its walls. My mother was fearful when she learned of this: What would the shtetl think? And in truth the shtetl women began to murmur "Lilith" when they saw her.

Unable to sleep, I worried. Miriam's song would enter my mind at night, when she was singing it and when she wasn't – the song seemed as much a part of me as of her, the only part of her that still was, but in an unwanted way, for I never felt myself singing it with her; she alone sang it in my mind, a song that divided us, that kept her separate from me.

In the family's desperation, the decision was made to consult the Tsaddik. When he sent for her, Miriam did not resist, walking to his residence beside me as unaware of my presence as when she walked at night, her shadow more real than the figure at my side. And it was precisely this conduct which was so remarkable and so frightening: Miriam did not resist our efforts to "cure" her (this was the word my mother used) but neither did she respond to them. Like wheat brushed with a stick, she yielded without yielding, and remained unchanged.

She did not resist when the Tsaddik led her into his study like a submissive bride. It was forbidden to listen through the door, yet I could not help doing so -- a former part of me – a part I despaired of regaining – was inside. Behind the closed door silence prevailed for the half hour that passed before I heard the Tsaddik's footsteps. I hurriedly retreated from the door, though it was not necessary; "Silence cannot be heard through a door," the Tsaddik said to me without anger, and in the same tone, "I can do nothing; she is beyond our help, for there is something that cannot be found in any place, not even with the Tsaddik, yet there is a place that there you will find it." His face was perplexed; Miriam's bore the same distant look as when she had entered.

Mother wept openly for twenty-four hours when I told her the words of the Tsaddik, as I wept inwardly for so much longer.

It was my uncle who suggested it. Not from a

willingness to help her as much as an attempt to get rid of her since, as one of the leaders of the community, he suffered from the shtetl's incessant talk of Miriam's "condition" – and implicitly, the lack of anyone's doing anything about it – more than the rest of the family. "Surely the place hinted at by the Tsaddik is the Land of Israel. Perhaps the climate there will aid her," he said, as if she suffered from tuberculosis. Even I chose to think of Miriam's condition as an illness: it removed the volition from our separation. The Land of Israel was espoused by the Lovers of Zion, and though my uncle did not hide his disapproval of the youth going there, in my sister's case – for reasons of health – he was willing to make an exception.

My mother reluctantly agreed, at panic's end about her daughter. I, too, was willing to seize at any hope, any chance, to reunite my sister to me. I was given the task of taking Miriam to the Land of Israel, to one of the settlements in the Galilee where sun and work would be allowed to heal.

The settlement caused a slight improvement, if an improvement only in body, not in mind. She became physically healthier – so that she worked during the day rather than slept and continued her night walks, now with the strength to do both. I, too, had benefited. The pain of estrangement from my sister was not lessened, yet I was no longer kept awake by her song. I was dimly aware of it, but it remained below the surface, only occasionally troubling me with its seductive melody.

Otherwise there was no change: Miriam remained apart from me, and from the settlers, an isolation they accepted; they were tolerant of an individual's habits so long as he or she was a good worker. If they wondered about her night wanderings and singing, they said nothing, for this was a peaceful time and there was then no hostility with the Arabs in neighboring villages to render her excursions dangerous.

It was to one of these villages to which she would walk, singing her song, as I learned from following her. Not an Arab village, but a village of Yemenite Jews near the Sea of Galilee. In the village she would stop before a certain house, no different from the houses surrounding it. She would stand gazing at it for long periods as if waiting for someone to emerge, but no one emerged, nor did she enter. The inhabitants sleeping inside seemed unaware of her presence, all the more so the other villagers. If they saw her on occasions when I did not follow her, I had no knowledge. Perhaps, like the inhabitants of the shtetl, they thought her an evil spirit and remained behind locked doors when she approached. When I did not follow her, I knew it was to this same house that she went. I envied the house the attention of Miriam that had once been mine.

For I was no closer to her without whom I only half-existed. My despair increased as the possibility of being reunited to her seemed ever more remote, since she continued to treat me with the same indifference she showed to other members of the settlement. Suicidal thoughts tormented me. If I could have been sure that my death would have caused her to shed even one tear – I would have taken my life. Doubting, I did not act.

During the second year that we dwelled in the Land of Israel, at the fall season of harvesting the apple crop, there occurred a slight change in Miriam. She became less remote from everyone in the settlement, except that her remoteness from me persisted. She spoke a bit more, and her secret – for the settlers suspected that she kept some secret – seemed less burdensome. There was now an expectancy about her, and a tension as if caused by her straining toward it, the effort of which pulled her partially free of her somnolence.

One night after dinner, as I lay back watching the stars, thinking how different they were from the stars above the shtetl – the ones my sister and I used to follow, tracing the constellations with our eyes and thought and laughing our conspiratorial laugh whenever we came to the Twins – my sister approached me in her silent way. Concentrating as I was that moment on tracing Aquarius, I was not immediately aware of her presence. When I sensed her standing there, I jumped up, amazed at this first sign of recognition after so long, my heart beating so strongly I felt like a lover who first sees his beloved after an intolerable absence. I was about to reach out to her, to gather her to me, when her hand on my shoulder stopped me, so gentle her touch that I was grateful for it alone. But it was her expression, the same a fawn has when it is listening for something, that prevented me from attempting to bridge a gap greater than separated me from the stars. And then I, too, heard he song. It did not come from Miriam, but from a flute somewhere out in the darkness, distant, the sound growing louder as its source approached.

Miriam turned to face it as if expecting it, looked back at me for an instant – then her face became submissive again and she moved in her silent pavan toward the sound. The figure playing it appeared, his face dark, his features not recognizable in the moonless night. He stopped as she approached him, turned, still playing, the two shadows merging into one glided down the path toward the village. I took a step toward them, toward my twin who was not my twin, but a slight movement of her finger stopped me. I knew she would not hesitate this time outside the house in the village. I knew, too, as I felt the song being pulled out of me forever, that in fusing her soul with another's, she had freed my own.

The Thirteenth World

The Tale of Rabbi Loew ben Bezalel and the Golem which he created is well-known. Less known are the variations of the tale. Still less known the variation you are about to hear. For if God is the Master of this world of worlds, he is also Master of the other worlds of which this world is one.

What is known is that on the 20th of the Hebrew month of Adar (the year is in dispute), Rabbi Loew succeeded in creating a Golem by the power of the esoteric knowledge contained in the Sefer Yezirah, the mystical Book of Creation: the words and letters of the Hebrew alphabet and the primordial numbers and the names of God. But what is not known is that Rabbi Loew made more than one attempt before succeeding. How else explain the rumors of mounds of clay found in the attic of the "old synagogue," so diverse in form that a Golem made from all of them would presumably be too patch-worked to function at all, and would collapse like the Tower of Babel. Is it surprising that Rabbi Loew had to try a number of times before succeeding? For is it not said that the Creator Himself created the world 26 times and only on the 26th time did it stand?

The place of the Golem's creation is not in dispute: the attic of the old synagogue in the city of Prague, in the ghetto of that city. Nor the is reason for the Golem's creation: the threat of pogrom to the Jews of the ghetto. The Sefer Yezirah contains the 22 letters which are the elements which lie at the basis of everything created; the letters that Rabbi Loew will use to create his Golem.

Miraculously, the doves that roost in the eaves of the old synagogue and the mice who live there have not tasted of the mounds of clay. On the ancient floor, each step of Rabbi Loew generates an echo that reverberates like thunder. The window panes are crooked and distort the shadows, forming strange forms on the floor. A dove's leg is transformed into a giant hand, like that of . . . a Golem.

And it falls upon Rabbi Loew to make this creature. If what we call "normal" is an awesome equilibrium, how much more awesome is the equilibrium required to create the non-normal. No one realizes this more than the rabbi, gifted in mathematics and astronomy as well as Kabala. At first he seeks the easy way out. From a dove, yes, it is handy, and it already breathes; a few changes here and there, -- and success. He searches the Sefer Yizerah for a hint of how to go about it. He begins to repeat all kinds of holy words concerning invoking doves. Ultimately he fails. His dove-man is a lump with rudimentary limbs neither arms nor wings, but something in between. Tears come to Rabbi Loew's eyes. But there are still the mice, perhaps even more man-like than doves. Again chanting. The result is a kind of large Sphinx-like mound of mouse-colored clay. Rabbi Loew chides himself that he is no better than King Rudolf's alchemist.

The rabbi steeps himself in the Sefer Yezirah and extracts from it what he believes is necessary to create a Golem. Yet he waits for a sign. He dreams that he visits the first world created which does not resemble our world at all. It is a kind of rough ball of clay and water, far from solid. He wakes from his dream, troubled. He rushes to the attic of the synagogue and at once he recites the chant based on what he has extracted from the Sefer Yezirah, standing above but to the side of a circle he has drawn on the wooden floor of the attic. His forebodings according to the dream are correct. A small shapeless lump of clay, the size of a homunculus, with perhaps the hint of a head results. He does not dare follow the next step, the writing of the required word "truth" on the forehead, for there is no forehead, and there is no man shape. He knows he has failed. Sorrowfully, with a trembling hand, he writes the word "death" (met) on the upper part of the form. It crumbles into small pieces of clay. He does not know if he is permitted to dispose of it, so he sweeps the pieces into a corner: let them be a reminder to him that, should he succeed, he is not The Creator, but only a minor creator, himself made in His image.

He continues to wait for a sign. The next night, he dreams once again, a dream of the sixth world created, it is more formed than the world of his last dream, possessing rough land areas surrounded by ocean, but uninhabited. He wakes, and half-hopefully repeats the process to create a Golem. This time the clay creature is larger, almost the size of a man, but as incompletely formed as the world in his dream. No utterance of the rabbi completes him. Once again he must write "death" on the form's uppermost portion, even if this time his hand trembles less, and he sweeps the resulting crumbled parts into a corner next to the remains of the first attempts at the Golem, the dove and the mouse. The words come to him: I slay and revive. He takes it as a sign of hope.

The next night Rabbi Loew dreams yet again. We should not be surprised. Does not the Zohar say: the borders between heaven and earth, logic and dream, are constantly blurred? So is the border between past, present, and future for the kabalist. Like his other dreams, this dream deals with the previous creations of the world attempted by The Creator before the final one. An earth of clay metamorphising, of clay being worked , and of the number 13, luminescent, being prominent. And one thing additional: a creature, seemingly Adam, the first man, in rough form, lacking a soul, a Golem. On waking, Rabbi Loew realizes: his Golem must come from this 13th world, a world that perhaps continues to exist parallel to his own world, perhaps does not, but exists or existed (for in the mystical world the past, present, and future may co-exist); it is from this world, he is convinced by his dream, his Golem must be brought.

But how? Aware of the dangers involved, he again reads and rereads the Sefer Yezirah in an effort to find the world or worlds needed to create his Golem. Rabbi

Issac Luria said that the line of division between the holy and the satanic is as thin as a hair. And there suddenly comes upon him from the future the words of Rabbi Nachman: if the eye could look into the mysteries of the body, of flesh and blood, it would see that upon every vein and muscle there hang worlds. But which world? Is it indeed the 13th?

After praying for guidance, the rabbi sways back and forth and begins to chant. The words he chanted to bring forth the Golem from the 13th world, we do not know. It may be reasonably assumed that they were the combination of Hebrew letters from the Sefer Yezirah, certainly the letters of the Name of Names, together with variations on the number 13. His words are directed upward to the Source of all creation and then downward to the floor, focused on a circle he has drawn with his forefinger dipped into a glass of ancient, dark red wine, so dark that it approaches the black of the stripes of the prayer shawl draped about his shoulders. He remembers the words of the Sefer Hayim: "From the dust under the constellation of stars man is created, and from the dust under the constellation of the Lion the beast is created." And it is for him to create a being in between the two: a Golem. He is tense, with the tension with which the act of creation tempts the creator, and more so with respect to the results of the process. Poised for the hint of something gone wrong, a ladder at the ready in case the Golem should be created not as he intended, and he should have to reach the creature's forehead to erase the Hebrew letter alef from emet (truth), leaving the word met (dead) in order to return the Golem to dust.

A small lump of clay suddenly appears and grows into a lump larger than a man's size, three cubits in length, in the rough form of a man lying, perhaps similar to that of Adam, the first man, when he was created. Or perhaps, indeed, Adam, the unfinished first man, without a soul, a model for the Adam of the Garden of Eden who came fully formed to the 26th world, our world. Rabbi Loew stares, full of faith and yet fearful, almost unbelieving that such a thing can occur. Now the form has limbs, a head; eyes form, followed by lips and hair. Even teeth, crooked like the window panes of the synagogue and leaning one upon the other like the gravestones of the ghetto's cemetery – Rabbi Loew cannot decide if this is a good sign or a troubling one. The figure is still inert, sleeping. The rabbi looks at it with tenderness and some horror. Rabbi Loew must wake him and instill in him the spirit of life. He hesitates, then with a look upwards, as if silently beseeching through the attic's roof He who is above, he dips his finger into the glass of wine, over which he has recited a blessing, and writes with a steady hand the Hebrew word for "truth" on the form's brow. The Golem's eyes open, his mouth utters one word: "Master". Rabbi Loew has succeeded. The savior of the Jews of the ghetto is ready to arise.

The Shoemaker

It was soon known in the neighborhood that the shoemaker had left his wife and children. Rumors abounded as to why and where he went. Varied and imaginative they were -- even that he went to look for the hidden place of the Ark of the Covenant. All of the rumors placed him in the desert because the reported sightings had him heading south. But exactly where in the desert, no one agreed. Some placed him in the caves near Qumran -- perhaps because his wife said that shortly before he disappeared, she heard him murmur over and over: "The wars of the children of light against the children of darkness." Others placed him in the cliffs above Ein Gedi.

His wife, who was known to refer to him even before he abandoned her, as "the crazy one," after a year met a man, moved in with him and, after

another year without a sign of her husband's returning, married him.

Three years later the shoemaker returned, indif-
ferent to his wife's remarriage, and ignored his
children whom his wife had raised to avoid him. He
angrily dismissed any questions as to his whereabouts
during the previous three years; in any event because
of his quick to anger temperament, few dared ask him
where he had been, or what he had done there. Even
the most persistent of neighborhood busybodies knew
to hold their peace in the presence of the shoemaker.
The saying, "If you don't want to be the sole of a shoe,
don't antagonize the shoemaker," was common neighborhood coinage. He was always "the shoemaker," as if
to use his name was too personal, evincing a familiar-
ity that could be dangerous. I called him -- to myself
– "Enoch" because of the legend of Enoch the shoemaker who with every stitch connected the upper
and lower world. There was something about him of
a prophet of wrath – except that he didn't prophesize.
Or if he did, we failed to grasp his prophecy.

Upon his return, the shoemaker shooed the cats
out of their quarters and reopened his cobbler shop
which had remained closed during his absence. No
longer with access to his former living quarters, he

slept on a mat on a narrow, raised platform he had built above his work bench. The shoemaker didn't have many costumers, either because of his strangeness or because of his temperament or because he was far from being a master of his craft, and the customers that did frequent his shop did so because it was located close to where they lived. Most of all, his prices were low.

From time to time, I gave him some business because I was curious about him and because I was drawn to the odor of leather and glue that filled the shop. He didn't mind if I lingered there without saying much. He usually had some tacks in his mouth, more, I suspected, as a defense against having to speak than as a work convenience. I didn't pester him with questions, adopting his strategy of silence, or indifference, which didn't help me much, even though he tolerated, and eventually seemed to even enjoy, my presence. Maybe he just got used to me—like an old shoe.

One day, as he was working on the sole of my shoe, he uttered, more to himself than to me, " 'And ye shall tread down the wicked, for they shall be ashes under the soles of your feet,' ", his hammering punctuating his avowal. And then he stopped, dropped his hammer, spit out the tacks (an act which surprised and startled me), and began mumbling something about the Rabbi from – he couldn't pronounce the name very well -- one of those towns in Eastern Europe. An uncommon rambling on the shoemaker's part about a rabbi who one day astounded his disciples by entering his room and refusing to leave it for the rest of his life, dependent upon them to bring him food. Here the shoemaker paused as if wrestling with some thought and then, holding my glance in his, added something about how the presence of evil in the world might possibly have been too much for the rabbi's sanity to bear. " 'Trapped in a fortress of evil without anyone to ransom him.' "

I nodded and said nothing. What could I say?

Some days afterward, the shoemaker was gone again. A second time. The desert again? No one knew. Speculation nourished the neighborhood gossip in the following days. Someone said that before he left, he murmured over and over, "Dispersed to the place of the wicked to their subduing by fire."

Toward the end of the same week, I heard a knock on my door. A youth stood there, a pair of shoes in his hands. "From the shoemaker ," he said. "I didn't leave him any shoes to be repaired," I told him. "He said they were a gift," the youth persisted. I glanced at the size written faintly inside the left shoe -- it was my size. Although they had been polished to a bright sheen, the shoes were not new, and I surmised that somebody had left them to be repaired and failed to pick them up. But why look a pair of gift shoes in the mouth? They were expensive shoes. The shoemaker's from better days? Maybe his wedding shoes? I thanked the lad and gave him some change. As he was about to leave, I grabbed his arm. "Tell me, do you know where the shoemaker went? His shop is closed." The boy shrugged, perhaps already thinking of what candy to buy with the coins I had given him..

I didn't get around to putting on the shoes for a couple of weeks, until my usual pair sprung a hole in the sole of one. As I put on the right shoe, I spied something inside. It was a folded piece of paper, which had been inserted in the toe portion of the shoe. On it was written a single word: "Azaz." I repeated the word over and over, trying to fathom what it meant, this shoemaker's code delivered in a shoemaker's fashion. Finally, it rang a bell. Something about a scapegoat.

The "Azaz" wouldn't let go of me. It was as if the shoemaker was pushing me to use the clue he had vouchsafed me to solve the mystery of his disappearance. I began to delve into the subject.

I had been right about the scapegoat connection. The scapegoat was a goat that carried the sins of the people placed on it, designated "for Azazel," which was driven onto the desert to perish as part of the ceremonies of the Day of Atonement. The rabbis of the time interpreted "Azazel" as "Azaz", which meant "rugged" and "el", which meant "strong". They considered that "Azaz" referred to the rugged mountain cliff from which the scapegoat was cast down. Others said it referred to the goat-like spirit haunting the desert to which the Israelites were accustomed to offering sacrifices. The shoemaker had had a wispy, goat-like beard. Surely coincidence, but I found it disturbing nonetheless.

I never saw the shoemaker again. Nor did anyone else. Perhaps his one word message meant that he hadn't yet given up the search for the key to the presence of evil and his beholding with his own eyes "the recompense of the wicked." I was not a type to go on quests, even though the nature of evil often confounded me. Although it is forbidden to feel envy toward a poor, lost shoemaker, I felt envy: I had to live with the vexatious question of evil; the shoemaker had gone to try to decipher it and strive with it.

When I wake up at night and cannot sleep, the bad

thoughts come. And so I, too, ponder the nature of evil in the world. Maybe for the shoemaker the days and the nights had become one.

Rashi said: "Satan prosecutes in the hour of danger" – that is, at such a time of danger he doesn't differentiate between the just and the wicked. Perhaps the shoemaker realized that the evil in himself or his attempt to uproot it impelled him to be alone in the desert. To be "subdued by fire" or to be "a brand plucked out of the fire." The Ramban said that just as the fire intended to destroy the thorns gets out of control and destroys the crops, the evil inside of us must be restrained.

The shoemaker was not a person of restraint.

For days the shoemaker and his quest weighed heavily upon me. It did not lift until shortly before the Day of Atonement when I chanced (if chance it was) upon the story of how one day Rabbi Levi Yitzhak was asked by a poor shoemaker if he had something that needed fixing. The rabbi chastised himself, "You see, even he can see that I need to fix myself."

Which may explain why I continue to bring my shoes for repair to shoemaker shops outside of my neighborhood when it would be easier to buy a new pair of shoes.

After the Revolution

THEY HAD PLANNED THE TRIP TOGETHER. A long-earned vacation. But before they could take it, Sadie had gone. And with her gone, the taste had gone out of it. He had put off going alone, but it was now or not at all. Soon he would be unable to make even such a short trip as this, short in distance but long in planning and he owed it to Sadie's memory, to himself.

As he watched the white wake of the ship in the blue somewhere between Miami and the Bahamas, he smiled, remembering the Wolfson play about the ferry-boat trip of idealists who set out from Brooklyn to sail to Russia in order to build the new world – and who never got out of the bay. The ultimate irony for them (as for him) who in those days believed that they were being carried on the wave of the future. The wave had broken without the future. Only the later freedom marches in the American south had salvaged something. Of the red and the black, the black had been successful; from the red only the afterglow of what might have been.

How different from the ringing words of the socialist hymn, 'The Internationale': "This is the final struggle."

So gloriously naïve had been their idealism. They had thought of the working class – how did someone describe it? – as composed not of miners, plumbers, and working men, but as a statuesque giant standing on a high hill facing the sun.

To face the sun these days hurt his eyes. He was better off at facing the sea. He almost turned to bestow this observation upon Sadie, but Sadie wasn't there anymore, and the charm she found, as she once said, in the self-effacing humor of a revolutionary now had no one to appreciate it.

They had participated tougher in the years of the civil rights struggle, even facing the dogs held by the troopers. Birmingham? … the old memory was beginning to slip.

Spain remained more concrete. But he had been young then. Heady days followed by heartache. That British chap had said it all. Only he should have titled his book Homage to Heartache.

The sunlight flecked off the water. The strains of the steel band lulling him into semi-sleep, as he leaned on the rail, the ship's motion merging into the memory of a play about another ship on which the voyagers only gradually realize that it is taking them, having died, on their final journey.

Once more that other journey of the past seeking the future intruded as words bubbling up from some buried repository: "We threw ourselves toward the future with too much passion ... we lost the feeling for the present . . .the ligature of time was torn." The ligature of time ... Sadie ... the liga – he was jolted back to the present by the music, louder now, played on the tops of oil drums by the musicians, the catchy rhythm blending absurdly with the words of the old song, "Arise for the day is coming" ... Past discontinuance, he thought, watching the water trail back to the past. And now to the syncopated, happy beat of the drums there came, incongruously, that other theme: "There are few of us now, soon there will be none ..."

He squinted at the eternal blue sky, so oblivious. The young people were dancing on the deck, drinking the rum-laced tropical drink, the "specialty of the house." He chuckled, recalling the libation sought by his group of young people: "O Russian proletariat . . . I long to share your meager bowl of kasha . . .". Only the white wake echoed Russian snows, echoed the white Russian-style blouse that Sadie wore when he first met her, echoed the white froth around the mouth of a comrade shot down next to him in the bright Spanish sun…

He shook his head, then looked up quickly to see if anyone was watching this old man with his memories. No one was watching, which disturbed him almost as much as if someone had been.

Ahead of the ship there appeared the flat land of the Bahamas. And with it, Whitman:

I will make divine magnetic lands,

With the love of comrades,

With the life-long love of comrades.

Whitman he had loved more than Marx. That first evening, he had confessed as much to Sadie. She had laughed. Rosa Luxemburg she wasn't. He was the heavier one. She the lass that lighteth his load. How lucky he had been. He tried to remember if he had told her how much she had meant to him. He couldn't remember. The loss of memory is worse than the loss of life. Perhaps Marx had made that discovery too.

He shook himself out of it. He was on "vacation." The black laborers moored the ship. He tried to see with what kind of knot . . .knots he had been taught by a counselor at the summer camp in which each bunk-house bore the name of a union, "The Brotherhood of Sleeping Coach Workers," "The ..." he couldn't resurrect them now. His eyesight could discern the knot, but not the type. "Well, that is still something," he sighed.

On shore, he wandered quickly through the international bazaar – each shop selling products from a different country. "An 'Internationale' of sorts, even if capitalistic. He drifted toward the hotel area, fanning himself with a brochure from one of the shops. One hotel constructed like an Eastern palace, a kind of Caribbean Taj Mahal, took his fancy. He sat in its splendid lobby. Sadie would have liked it; she had a taste for the rococo.

Suddenly he stiffened against his cushioned chair. He had been so absorbed in his thoughts that he hadn't noticed: Blacks, American tourists, made up most of the guests! Strolling around, happily, well dressed, on vacation! In the south he had seen their frightened faces as they (as he) had been beaten by the troopers. Those Blacks had seemed poor. He remembered the field workers seen from the bus traveling south. They had waved, seeing the bus with its northern license plate and knowing its purpose. But their faces had been wan. And now their children were here, in this setting more resplendent than the vowed hope of a Langston Hughes poem! Ah, Paul Robeson, if only … He felt a tug at his heart, a palpitation, and he feared the possibility of a heart attack. He took a deep breath. So it all hadn't been in vain after all. Not completely. If the world hadn't been transfigured, there were parts of it that had.

Maybe the ferryboat had brought him here to allow him to give a Bronx cheer to the boatman when he came to ferry him to the other side, should he cock a derisive eye at his life.

An observation he would have liked to make to Sadie.

The Wonder Hitter

HE DID NOT HAVE THE BUILD associated with a home-run hitter. He was plump in a youthful way, attractive rather than handsome, with a beautiful singing voice which he would exercise in private and occasionally in the dressing room after a game. Sometimes during his singing, his voice would waver strangely, and he would suddenly enter into an ecstatic trance, only returned to his taciturn normality by a cold shower. He possessed a changeable character, marked by fits of deepest gloom vying with moments of exaggerated joy. Sometimes he doted on company; mostly he sought isolation.

Yet when he stepped up to the plate, bat in hand, his face grew rosy, even glowing; it was then that he was capable of unprecedented feats. Once, still in the minors, he hit four home-runs in a game, thereafter carried from the ballpark on the shoulders of the fans. "The Messiah of Mobile," they hailed him; deservedly, he had saved the season for the hometown team.

Even then in the minors, he was a person apart, as if in exile from everyone and everything but the game, a tendency which increased when the Mets called him up. A Jewish slugger for New York seemed like a bestowal of divine providence. "His time has come," announced with quivering lips the Mets' coach, the electric Norton, to the press. The Mets were languishing in fifth place. Ted Sabin was immediately dubbed "The Savior" by the media and "Saving Sabin" by the fans, names he never denied. It was his skill with the bat which saved Sabin from being thought of as an 'oddball', though some called him eccentric. Eccentricity was an honorable tradition with the Mets.

He was uncanny. Opposing pitchers had long since exchanged "secret" information on how to get his number. Nothing helped – the baseballs continued to fly from his bat out of stadia as if propelled by a force not of this world.

His every move at the plate was studied from the moment that he entered the batter's circle until the completion of his marvelous swing. Invariably he touched the dust of the plate with the end of the bat before lifting it to his shoulder. The catchers strained to see what mark he had made. One even dared to ask him. "It's not a cross," he replied, the catcher unable to discern if in levity or seriousness. But Sabin was a hard guy to figure. Rumors told of a book he read constantly, thought to contain his secret. Still he inspired not scorn, but awe.

Some noticed that his lips moved or seemed to move imperceptibly before he swung the bat; others denied this, contending that he was simply moistening his lips or engaging in a nervous gesture; one more riddle in a game steeped in signs, arcane movements, masked meanings. That his face was illuminated everyone agreed, illuminated with – some described it as determination. One witness, a Baptist from somewhere in the Bible Belt, called it a nimbus, but this account is without authority as the describer, after a brief trial, was sent down to the minors. In baseball, as outside of it, the veracity of the tale depends on the authority of the teller.

Some attributed Sabin's success to his ability to read the signs given by the catchers, although he stood in front of them when at bat. Especially his ability to discern the four-fingered sign for a fast ball. Ballplayers are famous for their devotion to the mysterious.

Even the faithful Norton (a man said to almost worship Sabin), who had kept an eye on him from his earliest days in Mobil, was once heard to confess that Sabin was unfathomable. "Like no player I ever knew," the words attributed to him. The closest he came to defining Sabin took place on a shimmering hot August afternoon when Sabin hit two home-runs at each end of a double-header. "He isn't a natural," he explained to a sportswriter, "he seems to will home-runs. "Maybe," jibed the scribe, "it has something to do with that rain-bow." The rainbow in question, of brief but brilliant duration, hung beyond centerfield like an epiphany.

Norton was tight-lipped about only one aspect of Sabin's: his periods of depression (his periods of ela-tion disturbed Norton but did not worry him). Prone to depression himself, Norton knew its danger; in battling Sabin's depression, however, he had largely escaped his own -- a fact realized only years later, when Sabin was a legend, if a failed one. No, not failed, only, somehow, a fallen one.

No one ever knew (not even Norton who was closest to him, to the extent that anyone could be) that what Ted Sabin's mouth uttered just before he swung the bat was the forbidden Tetragrammaton. Nor that he desired devoutly a home-run, not to win ballgames for the Mets, nor the home-run championship for himself, nor even to justify Norton's faith in him, but in order to circle the bases: to complete by act the four-based manifestation of the utterance, the ultimate substantiation of the emanation of the Name. Only in this way could he prove himself.

After each game he would disappear, as though he regretted his success at the plate; but before the next game he returned, full of renewed enthusiasm. What part Norton played in his renewal can only be conjectured.

His fans of course knew nothing beyond the fact of his prodigious powers in the batter's box. He had taken the country by storm, had become the property of the many, his name hosannaed at every stadium in the nation. In New York, city of his team, he was king. At the moment of his fabulous swat, of the eighteen players on the field, seventeen were frozen in tableau, he alone moved in a whirlwind, as if time itself were frozen and he were outside of time.

Sabin had in the year that was to be his apogee approached the home-run record. At the season's midpoint he had thirty. Two months later, he had reached fifty-eight, Greenberg's feat. It was not until the final game of the season, that he tied the legendary Ruth's record with a clout that caused the ball to seem to ascend to heaven itself, swallowed in the pale radiance over mid-center. But in order to break the record, he would have to hit a home-run his last time at bat.

During his last time at bat, thunder and lightning were heard and seen despite the pure blue sky, a mystery not explained to this day, nor that of the bunting draped on the third base stands being rent at the same moment. The count reached two and two. Hushed were the stands as if in witness of a sacred ritual, as if the batter was about to confront the universe itself; the lower tiers plunged into darkness, as though in an abyss, redeemed only by the sparks of cigarettes; the higher tiers bathed in light. Everyone watching the figure who had crossed from the darkened portion of the field to the lighter part of the diamond to stand in a kind of interlineared splendor at the plate, the plate white as a shroud.

Against him, the pitcher, nervous but not without courage, caught up in a situation in which he could not purposefully walk Sabin, the bases being loaded, and he, blessed with a two run lead, in reach of his twentieth game win. He went to his best pitch, his fast ball. When he wheeled and released it, the ball seemed to leap forward toward the plate. Blazing it was, and true, dividing the plate with Manichaean precision.

Yet to Sabin, the ball seemed not to move at all. The sphere hung there like a sun standing still, a glowing wheel held in the radiance of eternity, suspended, waiting for him. Suddenly his lips went dry, he was not able to utter even the first letter of the Name. He stood in terror of it. The bat never left his shoulder. He seemed in a trance. The "strike three" call of the umpire, shouted along with his sign, the shriek of Norton, were subsumed in the silence.

Sabin retired from baseball, despite everyone's (not excluding the President's) efforts to reverse his act of apostasy and keep him in the game. Only Norton, to everybody's amazement, did not try to convince him. When asked why, he would only reply, as if privy to some great concealment, "It is his decision."

But was it?

Perhaps the time has not yet come to reveal the meaning of these things.

Sabbath Evening in Jerusalem

Sabbath evening in Jerusalem.
He repeated the words in time to his steps.
Sabbath evening in Jerusalem
It seemed a promise of something.
Sabbath evening in Jerusalem.

Sabbath candles were lit in each house he passed, some placed near the window, some upon white-clothed tables. The singing of the Sabbath songs, too, continued from house to house as he walked, "a bridge from generation to generation".

He was alone, but he was not alone; perhaps it is more accurate to say, he was alone but found a satisfaction in it.

Those singing had a warmer satisfaction: family, with all this word conjured up to the unmarried

Sabbath walker. His satisfaction was that of the outsider, the loner yet (and this he was careful to admit) the outsider who would one day be happy like the families he had passed: not walking outside, but sitting inside, singing, surrounded by the warmth of the Sabbath candles. This belief added a sense of hope that prevented his loneliness from being oppressive.

His was the loneliness that would be redeemed.

The cool, pure air of autumnal Jerusalem upon his face was softened from time to time by a warm breeze, perhaps from the Judean desert, a breeze which seemed to him feminine, and the thought of the Shekina slipped momentarily into his mind.

I will find her, I will find her, his steps said.

If I have not lost her, his steps answered, for this Sabbath evening he had glimpsed through a window a face which arrested him, the face of a young girl close to his age with downcast eyes. Perhaps she had just finished blessing the Sabbath candles. But no, that would have occurred earlier. On seeing her, he stopped. If only he could meet her (the thought had come to him clear and piercing), the rest would follow, as smooth and continuous as the Sabbath tablecloth, as unwavering as a sustained note. It was the initial step which was crucial. But he had not seized the opportunity by remaining outside the window. He feared he would frighten her. She had raised her head and looked at him and he had moved away, though it was equally possible (as he relived the event – the first of a thousand relivings) that she had not seen him at all. The house was illuminated and he would not have easily been seen in the darkness outside.

And what if she had seen him? Did he really believe that she would have miraculously taken pity on his Sabbath loneliness, flung open the door or even the window, taken his hand and drawn him inside as in some shtetl romance? Still he was convinced that if she had, the chain had only begun, he would at that very moment be seated next to her around the Sabbath table, and for all the Sabbaths to come, which he pictured as an infinite series of receding Sabbath tables.

Why didn't I wait, why didn't I wait?, his footsteps asked.

No longer did he see Sabbath tables before his eyes, but only the sidewalk stretching ahead of his feet as a sense of irreparable loss overwhelmed him, a loneliness no longer redeemable as it had been before seeing the girl through the window. Dark-haired, she had appeared to him as altogether lovely, as Anne

Frank might have appeared had she been allowed to grow up.

Afterward he had married—no, not to the girl in the window, not even a dark-haired girl, as it turned out. Sometimes, usually on Sabbath evening when his wife blessed the candles, he thought of the girl in the window, as if she had come to him carried on the breeze that often comes before sunset in Jerusalem. He tried to recreate her face – was she really as pretty as he had thought? How many times in his life had he considered a girl pretty at first glance, and later adjusted his opinion, as if hope had given way to reality, or perhaps simply aware of the fact that he couldn't have her? Even years later he upbraided himself for not remaining longer outside the girl's window; if nothing else, to focus on her eyes, on her chin, on her nose, to establish that she was not pretty – then he would not have been so saddened that she hadn't led him inside and sat him next to her at the Sabbath table.

Now as his footsteps beat out the rhythm "I have seen my Sabbath queen," she was fresh in his memory, pretty, and over the years would always be pretty because he hadn't had time to establish the possibility of her not being so. Her black dress may also have been responsible. In blue or red, or even white, she might not have been pretty. And Sabbath and the candles (and his predilection for black dresses) may have all been responsible.

However much he loved his wife, and love her he did, he would feel a pang of loss whenever he thought of the girl in the black dress, but he couldn't know this yet on the night he had glimpsed her as his feet tapped out the increasing distance separating him from her forever. He would always be aware of how silly he was – if he had spoken to her, or she to him, he might have discovered that she was frivolous or a hundred other negative things. But he had not spoken to her, and she had not spoken to him, and so he continued to imagine her as warm and sweet, even as his wife was not unwarm and not unsweet. But he lived with his wife and not with the girl, whose intangible warmth and sweetness were unimpeachable; and while his wife did the dishes or did other mundane tasks, the girl stood forever in her black dress in the glow of the Sabbath candles, would stand there in his memory during the days of his life, and even at his death, he would remember her as he had seen her on that Sabbath evening, smile at the silliness of an old man, but cherish her nonetheless . . .

The Ukrainian Bride

Enough time has passed, so I can tell the story. And since I am married now, I can do so without my kishkes shrinking. To you I can tell it, a stranger on a train. That, too, is a literary tradition, Moshe Mocher Sefarim, Tolstoy. Get it off the chest to someone you will never see again. I cannot tell it to my wife – she might divorce me. Maybe I will make her a gift of it in honor of our tenth wedding anniversary.

I married late, like everything else I do. When I was thirty-eight, forty staring me in the face like the abyss, I despaired of finding a wife and starting a family. I had had my chances – my 'almosts', but in the end, no chupah. Thoughts of giving up the search in favor of escaping to a monastic life tempted me: uniform dress, a narrow bed, a simple wooden chest of drawers, shoes under the bed.

Alas, there were no Jewish monasteries. Back to square one.

At this nadir of connubial quest, I read the advertisement in the paper. A program for an all-inclusive, round-trip flight to the Ukraine and introduction to a prospective bride. Ridiculous of course: this wasn't the American Wild West of mail-order brides, but during the days that followed, the idea gnawed at me. "Last Chance Gulch" repeated itself like a mantra in my head. "What have you got to lose?" I asked myself. "Pay the $4,000, fly to the Ukraine, meet the 'bride', and see if you can hit it off." Opposites attract, nu?

There was even a certain 'romantic' component to the idea. Our kids would ask how mom and dad met. I would hem and haw, and say something about our meeting abroad, and their mother would say, laughingly, "Your father purchased me in the Ukraine." She would say this if she possessed a sense of humor, and if she didn't, she wouldn't have become my wife. Me, I had a sense of humor -- how otherwise would I have participated in the ridiculous caper? In truth, like so many crazes and fads in Israel, the era of the Ukrainian shidduch was short-lived: a number of Israelis gave it a try, bringing back their brides, but the marriages were of limited duration, due to differences

in mentality, difficulty in adjusting to a new country, and age differential (some Israelis of mature age
wanted to bring back a young bride to make their
friends jealous). Also the brides couldn't adjust to the
stringent culinary demands of the Israeli mothers-in-
law, usually surrounding the precise cooking needs of
their sons (Moroccan cuisine and Ukrainian cuisine
partaking of some differences).

During the flight to the Ukraine, dozing, I dreamt
of a woman with pomegranate-like breasts standing
with outstretched palms, whose source I identified
on waking as that of a statue of Diana of Ephesus.
Anyhow, full of hope mixed with trepidation (appropriate to one who got nervous on every single blind
date, despite the many I had gone on in an attempt to
find 'the one', albeit that this madcap adventure was
the mother of blind dates), I found myself in a kind
of inn-cum-singles-bar, whose rustic, primitive charm
would have won the hearts of pioneers of the second
aliya, ensconced in a town with an unpronounceable
name, like the goyishe towns in the stories of Shalom
Aleichem..

Sitting there, awaiting my 'bride' with trepidation,
I almost bolted, returning home to Israel ready to tell
my friends that I had gone to Rumania to try my luck

in a casino. What kept me immobile was the worrying phrase that repeated itself over and over in my head: 'Drinking in the last-chance saloon' which alternated with the Proverbial encouragement, 'Find a wife, find a good thing' (which an exegete no less than Edgar Allan Poe thought originally was 'Find a good wife, find a good thing').

And then I saw her. All thoughts of leaving evaporated. A sheyne meydel, indeed. What caught me, even more than her raven-black hair -- worn Ukrainian style in a modest braid circling the crown of her head like a halo -- was her blue eyes which shown with an inner radiance like those in icons of Christian saints. I thought at first that a woman of such fair and spotless beauty was being led by our intermediary (shadchan didn't fit, somehow) to another table, to another 'groom', if a handsomer one, who had parted with $4,000 for the honor. I almost panicked as she was brought to my table, eyes downcast..

The go-between introduced us in English -- our lingua franca - with a certain nonchalance which surprised me, but for which I was grateful. Maybe he spied my state-of-shock stare, or the beads of cold sweat which I sensed had broken out on my forehead. The introduction completed, he left us alone: me and

Helena, the prospective groom and bride. I played with the knot of my tie (a rare sartorial accoutrement, in honor of the occasion). One thing in her favor, she had pointed to herself as she was introduced to me and her name spoken. There was something charming in this gesture, her delicate hand white as that of a marble statue, though she looked as if she was about to faint.

We sat staring at one another. The rooster and the hen. A good title if Shalom Aleichem would recount these events. Did my Helena know who Shalom Aleichem was? No, don't rush things.

I couldn't help wondering, as she stared at me, if she had ever seen a Jew, or an Israeli before. She blushed (charmingly, how charmingly), for which I was grateful. I half expected her to make the sign of the cross over the twinned onion-domed cupolas which pressed so fetchingly against her long-sleeved blouse.

Her English was as good as mine. This both pleased and disturbed me. I don't remember what we talked about, small talk surely. Assuredly nothing about the 'match.' She was reticent – something about her was vulnerable, or spiritual, virginal even. We drank tea (I feared beer would send the wrong message, let alone something stronger, which I could have sorely used), she barely sipping.

Now according to the scenario as it had been explained to me, if things went well, we would undergo a short marriage ceremony, Ukrainian style, and, if she agreed to it, she would become my wife, and I could take my Ukrainian bride back to the Promised Land. Apparently the ceremony was du rigueur to forestall mere sexual liaisons or was required by Ukrainian law or to please the bride's family. In any event, I was not interested in a one-night stand followed by an excuse for non-compatibility. I wanted a wife.

Helena was so vulnerable, so spiritual, that I quickly made clear to her I was looking for a wife and was not simply looking for a physical partner for a fling of limited duration at home or abroad. She seemed greatly relieved to hear this, which was not exactly flattering on the one hand, but on the other elevated her spiritually as a worthy spouse.

She was also pleased that a Ukrainian wedding would not take place. I explained to her that we would travel to Israel – she as my "guest," no strings attached – and if we turned out to be mutually compatible per-sonality-wise – then the physical "intimacy" would take place. Followed by a wedding, of course.

And so we dispensed with the usual three-day 'honeymoon' and, following a two hour excursion to the Shrine of the Blue Virgin, or Weeping Virgin (I forget which), an odd choice, I thought, flew to Israel or "the Holy Land", as she insisted on calling it to my discomfiture, as if an expression of non-recognition of Herzl's efforts.

My Helena hadn't taken me to meet her family, which surprised me, but then maybe they were hostile to the whole idea of their little dove being spirited away in the talons of the Levantine hawk, or perhaps she didn't think they would be impressed by me. The thought that she might simply want to escape the poverty then prevailing in the Ukraine came to me, yet she seemed too pure for such material machination. For my part, I was relieved I didn't have to spend a night under her parents' (thatched?) roof. She lived at home, which held a certain innocent charm in my eyes. I pictured her house as a rustic wooden structure with antlers hanging on the walls, another reason to be grateful for not having to spend the night under her roof, however ridiculous such musings were.

Home, in Jerusalem, she slept in my bed, I on the sofa, as per the oral ketubah (marriage contract) between us. I was disappointed at the lack of any romantic hints on her part. I bore it as the nazir (ascetic) I felt myself to be for the sake of the written ketubah to come, sustained by the memory of the doubly auguring moment when, on our way to visit to the shrine of the Virgin in the Ukraine, as a flock of trumpeting cranes flew overhead in a V (yes, for Victory) formation, Helena said softly, her uplifted blue eyes mirroring the pure blue of the sky, "Each bird has only one mate for life." I would have squeezed her hand in joy, but for it, together with the second, clasping a large bouquet of red flowers in front of her like a bridal bouquet, which she was bringing to the Virgin, perhaps a votive offering in thanks for our betrothal.

To mark her first day in her new country, I planned to take Helena on a tour of Jerusalem's sites: a fancy restaurant in the Mamilla mall followed by the old city stalls where she could shop to her heart's content. No, she wanted to see the Church of the Dormition of Our Lady on Mt. Zion and the Church of the Tomb of the Virgin Mary in the garden of Gethsemane (she had apparently prepared her itinerary in advance). A weird feeling suffused me as she genuflected and slowly made the sign of the cross on entering these shrines. She had done the same in the Ukraine -- but here in the Jewish State? I didn't want to raise a family of choirboys. Second thoughts began to assail me.

The second day it was the Via Delarosa – each station of the cross would bring on a new round of weeping. I tried to comfort her. "I am weeping in joy," she insisted, leaning on my arm increasingly at each station. Blessedly, at the Church of the Holy Sepulcher, I handed her over to the Arab guide, and found a bench to rest my weary bones.

After some days, my patience at Helena's lack of physical affection began to wear thin. She refused to kiss, and suffered my holding her hand as if I were holding a limp fish, which caused me to abandon this practice.

I had promised her while still in the Ukraine that I would pay for her return flight home if we didn't marry. When in pique at her lack of romantic ardor, I raised this subject, she replied that it wouldn't be necessary, she wanted to "dwell in the Holy Land". My hopes soared.

One night, she gave me a goodnight kiss (on the cheek) -- not much, but an improvement, even though I had the odd feeling that she would have kissed me on the forehead but for the fact that my tallness put it out of reach. A farewell kiss, as it turned out, because the next day she was gone, as I learned from the note in her childlike English script left on the table. A note in which she thanked me for bestowing on her "many kindnesses" which she would never forget, especially that of leading her on her "pilgrimage to the Holy Land" and her "destiny". No, she hadn't run off with a handsome rogue she had somehow contrived to meet, however unlikely the opportunity, since she had always walked in my shadow, eyes downcast. No, she had bigger fish to fry.

She had entered a convent! The Sisters of Our Lady of Zion (just off the Via Delarosa). As she explained it in her note, in order to become "a bride of Christ," a "consecrated virgin" (nu). Surely a step up from Zalmon-the bride-buyer-and-aspiring-virgin-deflow-erer (after marriage) -- but no, I didn't know whether to laugh or cry. She was surely the most beautiful nun in the convent.

I never told a soul about all this. Only my best friend knew the truth about my stations of the cross and I could trust him not to reveal them, especially as I had something on him from his early marital days that he wanted kept a secret. "Helena went back to her mother," I explained to the rest of the guys, unable to live down the nunnery part; I doubted they would stumble upon her in a convent – the Betar Jerusalem football team didn't play their games there. "Missed her terribly. An only child," I embroidered. "Actually she liked me, but her family ties were too strong." I almost convinced myself. "And she didn't like falafel," I added, as if putting a happy face on it.

A year later I met Malka. Malka was the opposite of Helena – lively, voluble, confident, the opposite of me, too. She had a real sense of humor, something that Helena completely lacked. Although I am sure that Malka would get a kick out of my tale, I don't want to look ridiculous in her eyes. I wouldn't hear the end of "my Ukrainian bride." No, not a gift to her for our tenth wedding anniversary, maybe on the twentieth, I will tell her. Or our fiftieth.

A recurring dream comes to me in which Helena leaves the nunnery, shows up on my doorstep and, raising her soulful eyes to my own amazed ones, palms outstretched, exclaims softly, oh so softly, "I made a mistake, maybe we –" then spies Malka and putting two and two together, begins to weep, making the sign of the cross over her heaving, enticing bosom. Never more than at that moment does her porcelain, suffering face remind me of that of Our Lady of Sorrows. As for me, I feel closer to Our Lady of Sighs.

You have to get off now? Your stop? I ask my listener on the train. Yes, an interesting experience. What? You think home-grown shidduchs are best? Could be. Shabat shalom to you, too.

Just before he left the train, he turned to me. "Perhaps your mistake was not taking her on a tour of Mea Sharim (the ultra-orthodox neighborhood)."

To this day I cannot decide if he was serious or kidding.

The Wonder-Worker

From the café that sat for years on the corner of the street which years later became a mall, Gershom spied his friend and companion, Franz, walk hurriedly by. Gershom shouted to him to come and sit over a tea and a Viennese. Franz seemed to hesitate, then sat. Gershom put his newspaper aside. "Conversation is preferable to reading the paper – cheerier," he said. Franz smiled wanly. "Nu," said Gershom. "What's troubling you?" Franz paused and then decided against confiding. "Everything's ok."

The waitress took Franz's order. Tea, as usual. He waved away Gershom's suggestion of a pastry to go with it. Gershom pointed to his empty glass of tea for the waitress to refill it. "Seen Jacob lately?" Franz asked. "Don't you know, he's in the hospital," replied Gershom. "Serious?" asked Franz. " Gershom shrugged. "He says it's nothing. Word has it otherwise." "We're all subject to checks," mumbled Franz. The waitress brought Franz's tea. After ten minutes of small talk broken by long silences, Franz glanced at his watch. "Got to go. Sorry," he said, standing. "But --" before Gershom could finish his protest, Franz waved him off, tapped his watch, and hastened to the waitress to pay his account.

"What are you, a secret agent in your old age?" shot Gershom as Franz hurried past him, but his friend had not heard, or feigned as if he hadn't.

When next saw Gershom saw Franz, it did not seem logical that he would be entering the premises of a wonder-worker. Gershom stared at the neglected entrance, the dilapidated building inside which 'The Piercing Light' dispensed charms for barren women, amulets for finding a husband, and cures for men and women. Gershom shook his head, even though in certain circles, stories of the wonder-worker's success were rife . Not his circles, of course. Nor Franz's. Franz, the old Franz, would never have entered. He was the first to condemn wonder workers as quacks. And yet he had seemed preoccupied the last time Gershom had seen him. Maybe he was ill. He had mentioned checks. Maybe the doctors hadn't been reassuring. Maybe

— but Franz, the central European educated rationalist, put himself in the hands of a wonder-worker? Never. He would prefer to die first.

A couple of weeks later, Gershom spied Franz at the café. A newspaper sat in front of him on the table. Franz ignored it, sat staring into space, and did not perceive Gershom until the latter waved a hand in front of his eyes. Franz smiled weakly. "Hello Gershom."

"Hello yourself." Instead of sitting as usual without need for an invitation, he asked Franz, "May I sit?"

"Of course," Franz said. "Since when do you need an invitation?"

Since I may have seen you become pals with a wonder-worker, Gershom said to himself. What he said was, "I wasn't sure."

Franz nodded. "I have been . . . preoccupied."

Gershom thought of the wonder-worker. "Your health?"

"It's ok – for my age. My problem is not physical."

Gershom raised an eyebrow.

Seeing his look, Franz sought to reassure him. "Not mental in the greater sense … in the lesser."

"Nu?"

A flock of birds passed noisily in the sky.

"Heading south," Franz said. "To Africa for the winter."

"A very interesting ornithological observation," commented Gershom dryly. "But I am more interested in Franz." After a pause, "What would send him to a wonder-worker?"

"Who?" exclaimed Franz, stunned. "How did you know?"

"Like so many other things—by chance. I thought I saw you a couple of weeks ago entering, ah, 'The Piercing" – he couldn't bring himself to utter the full title. "But I wasn't sure it was you."

"Rationally it wasn't. And yet rationally it was."

"I fail to follow."

"No, I don't want a baby and I don't have a tumor, so far as I know. But I did want something."

"Nu?"

"Justice."

"Justice? You are being sued?"

"No. Justice in a wider sense. Ultimate justice."

"And the wonder-worker could provide it?" He strove to pronounce this without irony.

"In a sense. If he can work miracles, he has God's ear, right?"

"Nu?"

"Which proves there is a God?"

"I suppose so."

"Ah, you see," Said Franz, leaning closer. "If God exists, he may punish."

"Yes…"

"Punish the Nazis. In the world to come. Reward the victims" He grabbed Gershom's arm. "That's why I went to him. To find justice."

Gershom cleared his throat. "And did you?"

"He told me to come again."

"And you are going?"

"Of course. There's too much at stake not to."

Slowly, Gershom stirred his cup of tea.

The Garden of Allah

WHEN THE NEW PATIENT WAS INSTALLED in the next bed, Frankel didn't pay much attention. Friendships in his ward were apt to be short-lived. As in the army during the war, you were not sure if it paid to get acquainted. Still, Frankel didn't feel like reading. It was too much of an effort lately. His eyes would tire easily, or he would get headaches. Speaking was less tiring.

He studied the man who now sat up in bed, staring around like a squirrel introduced to a new tree. A slight smile – friendliness, bemusement, diffidence, irony played about his lips. When his gaze met Frankel's, he nodded. Frankel nodded back. He felt sorry for the man. Not because he was in the hospital, but because he was new. Even in a hospital being used to a place was an advantage. The man looked to be of Eastern origin. It was when he, Frankel, said "shalom" and the man answered "shalom" more like "salaam" that he realized how Eastern: he was an Arab.

This fact made no difference to Frankel. Maybe once, not now. What mattered now was whether the man was noisy or a nudnik or stupid. The latter had nothing to do with education, but with character.

The man lay back, tired or hit by the realization of where he now found himself. He seemed oblivious of the stares of the others in the room. A new patient was always the subject of scrutiny, because he was new and because the others were curious as to the stage of his illness. Moribund patients cast a pall in the room. They also had difficult nights, which disturbed the others. And the deathbed scenes were uncomfortable – in themselves and because they were a rehearsal of the future: a play for which all the patients had a ticket, the only question being whether the performance would be sooner or later. Only the few lucky ones were able to go home to enjoy the luxury of attending a regular theater. That was for the younger ones with his "ailment," as he referred to it.

His name – the new patient's – was Mohammed. "What else?" mused Frankel, although his name wasn't so original either. "David," Frankel said, with the exchange of names. It was soon established that both had the same ailment – and in the same place. Mohammed had tapped his head; it was sufficient explanation. Frankel had replied with a similar gesture of explanation, although conscious of its comic aspect. My alter ego, he thought.

Mohammed spoke Hebrew; Frankel did not speak Arabic. He was the intellectual, yet they had to speak in his language as Mohammed did not know German or French. The thought galled Frankel. And so on the second day after Mohammed's arrival, Frankel, in his customary vigorous way, decided to do something about it. Leaning on one arm, he turned toward Mohammed. "Teach me Arabic."

Mohammed chuckled. "Learning Arabic takes time," he said in Hebrew.

"Time I have – I hope," said Frankel, also in Hebrew.

Mohammed laughed. He hesitated, shifting his body to a more comfortable position facing Frankel. "Why do you want to learn?" From another room the faint moans of a suffering patient could be heard. "I want to be able to talk to Allah in his language," Frankel answered.

And so the lessons began, interrupted by required ministrations, or fatigue, or the wheeling to the x-ray machine. The Arabic lessons were good for both of them. It lessened the need to talk of their situation. The only aspect that interested Mohammed was the x-ray machine, particularly the red light on the side of the machine. "It is such a lovely red. The color of wine in the garden of Allah," he said on one occasion. "Let us hope so," replied Frankel, in Arabic.

The proverbs were the best. Mohammed used them sparingly at first, but Frankel's delight in them encouraged Mohammed to produce more – when he could remember. Frankel, in his turn, instructed Mohammed in Yiddish proverbs, at first in Hebrew, and later – the simple ones – in Arabic. Mohammed was fond of "Shrouds are made without pockets." Frankel less so.

One morning Mohammed tried to speak and could not. Frankel was surprised at the instant of panic, then sadness this caused him, not only for Mohammed, but for himself: it meant the end of the lessons. A week later Mohammed was gone.

In one of those coincidences life seems to delight in as long as it can, another Arab took his bed. A younger man, jaunty despite his illness, self-assured, to Frankel a reproof of the older generation. He was known as "the smoker" because despite the prohibition, he persisted in smoking when the nurses weren't around. He probably wouldn't have had patience to teach Frankel Arabic even if Frankel had desired it.

But Frankel had no desire to learn Arabic any more.

Yeshiva Student

He did not stop as was his custom to read the notices pasted on the wall, not even one signed by the rabbinical council which denoted a matter of extreme importance. Once he would have devoured such a message – perhaps there would be a demonstration. For a respected yeshiva student like himself, one who drove himself to excel, demonstrations were a way of clearing his head, in addition to performing a mitzvah.

But today he did not even glance in the direction of the notices, ignoring their exhortations to read them via headlines and exclamation points and the vying colors of their paper. Today he walked rapidly, but not to the yeshiva: he had actually taken a day off from his studies because of the thought, the thought that had crept into his mind as if inserted by Sammael, "But what if it is not true?" Wherever he turned – morning prayers, evening prayers, the prayer upon going to bed, upon waking up – he heard a voice whisper, "But what if it is not true?"

He had never questioned his world. The world: Heaven and earth as set out in the Torah. He had delighted in it, nestling within the emanations of the Torah as within a quilt on a cold winter's night. Talmud allowed for questioning, but this was different. You questioned aspects of Torah, not Torah itself.

As he walked he strove to shut out the refrain, "But what if it is not true?" But how could it be not true – every man dressed in black like himself that he saw on the street, his street, attested to the truth of it. Men far wiser than himself – even the head of the yeshiva – labored in its service, as he himself had always striven to do. And now, even as he walked, the words mocked his movements, "But what if it is not true?"

He felt himself close to collapse. Greetings on the street went unacknowledged. If it were summer, he could have gotten away on a summer recess tour. Climb some hill, or travel a stream bed, and perhaps escape. But it was winter.

His walking brought him to the Western Wall at midnight. For a time, he prayed and the question did not assail him. But then it came, as if oozing from the very stones, "But what if it is not true?" Even here, he thought. More the profanation. He wrote quickly on a piece of paper, "Help me!", stuffed it in a crevice, and fled.

The next morning, he returned to his studies. Some of the students looked at him closely because he seemed agitated or because he had been absent the day before. "Are you all right?" asked Yonah, his study partner.

"No!" he sobbed. Yonah put an arm around his shoulder. "What is it, Moshe?"

"I can't tell you," Moshe said. "Let's continue."

Somehow, he got through the day, even though between the lines of the text he studied crept the words, "But what if it is not true?"

After studies had finished, Yonah sat on the bed across from him. "Do you want to talk about it?"

"It?" laughed Moshe a laugh of helplessness. "Yes, it. 'It' is the problem."

"What 'it'?"

"All of it," gestured Moshe helplessly. And then he burst out, "But what if it is not true?"

"What?" asked Yonah.

"Torah," whispered Moshe.

Yonah seemed to draw back physically, or did Moshe only imagine it? His friend thought for a moment. "But how can that be?"

"I don't know. That's what a voice says to me all the time. " 'But what if it is not true?'"

Yonah was silent for some moments. "You've been studying too hard, Moshe."

"But if it is not true, don't you see, it's all for nothing. All of it – the yeshiva, the synagogue, our clothes, our ways, everything."

"Why?"

"'Why'? How can you ask 'why?" he pushed past Yonah and ran from the building. It was raining. This surprised him. When he studied, he didn't pay attention to anything else.

He began to run as if pursued by Sammael. He ran, and the whispering voice 'But what if it is not true?' matched him step for step, seemed to cling to his racing heels. He ran down the narrow street, a narrow street in Jerusalem, but what could have been a narrow street in the Jewish quarter of Prague and a hundred other quarters, now or a century ago, or some centuries ago. He drew his coat over his head to protect himself from the stinging rain, and to keep from being recognized. There flashed through his mind the picture of the hassid in the tale who was ordered by a Messenger of the Lord to run from one village to another with his face covered with a prayer shawl so that no one would recognize him. On the third day he passed a man wrapped in a prayer shawl exactly like himself running in the opposite direction.

Moshe stopped inside a building entrance to catch his breath.

"You, there." The voice belonged to an elderly man with a disheveled grey beard flecked with brown. Moshe started. "It's all right," the man brushed his shoulder with his hand.

"Why are you running, young man?" he asked, scrutinizing Moshe. "Ah, I see."

"What do you mean?" Moshe stammered.

"I mean what I said. I see. Me'igra rama lebira amikta: 'From a high roof to a deep pit.' You have lost your faith."

Moshe stood dumbfounded, unable to utter a word. He had sought shelter and found instead a man who knew his innermost thoughts. Worse, his innermost fear.

"No, I am not Elijah. I simply have eyes. It is written on your face. You are not the first, you know."

Moshe didn't know. He looked toward the entrance, prepared to run.

The old man moved slightly, enough to block Moshe's path. "You can't escape lost faith by running. As Rebbe Nachman said, 'The edge of the void is never further away than a single false step.'"

Moshe leaned against the wall, feeling faint. "But what if it is not true?" he murmured.

A sad smile formed on the man's lips. "But what if it isn't ?. . . Torah is still the best of all worlds."

At these words, Moshe shivered. But now not from fear. From relief, like the last shiver of a fever beaten. The old man's words lightened his load. They had not removed it, but the difference was like balm to a wound. He wanted the man to continue, yet he was embarrassed to request it. "Are you a rabbi?" he asked.

His question was answered with a chuckle. "Every Jew is a rabbi, even if a small rabbi. You want me to continue" asked the man, deciphering his real question.

"Please," Moshe said.

"Suppose it is not true, young man." He paused and hunched his shoulders slightly. "It is still better than anything else."

"I do not understand."

Even if there is nothing but rock and gasses, stars and emptiness out there," the man seemed to gaze far beyond the doorway, "the beauty of Torah will still shine."

"But how? . . ."

"Torah is a way of life – a tree of life for those who grasp it. Torah is the best of what can be grasped. And if there are other beings on other planets capable of grasping, Torah would be best for them, too."

"Even if there were no . . .," his eyes glanced briefly upward.

"Perhaps even then, Heaven forbid."

Again Moshe stood dumbfounded. Yet freed of a burden. Tears of gratitude formed in his eyes.

"A tree of life to those who grasp it," the man repeated, grazing Moshe's shoulder with a sinewy hand.

"Yes, whispered Moshe. The voice of doubt had fled in confusion like Amalek before Moses.

He wanted to kiss the man's hand. "How can I ever repay you?"

A sad smile formed on the old man's lips; a smile that seemed a grasping in the face of the eternal. "Remember me," he said. After a few moments of silence, he added, "But you are not finished, young man. The rabbi from Kotsek once said, "If you feel pain, dance with it.' You still have to dance." Moshe wanted to ask him what he meant, but the man suddenly raised his prayer shawl over his head, perhaps against the rain, pushed past him, and hurried away, a dark figure merging with the dark weather and the grey streets.

Moshe stumbled out, weak yet replenished. He wondered if the kabbalists of old had felt like this following a night of mystical contemplation.

"Are you all right, Moshe?" asked Yonah on his return. "You look like you have seen a ghost."

"I am all right." He turned to the assigned tractate and began studying.

In the days that followed, the stabbing question had not returned – and yet he felt something still vexing him. Subtle, not like the voice, but nevertheless there, as if an echo of his previous doubt. This he could live with, Moshe thought, although he hoped that it, too, would disappear. Sometimes he thought of the old man's parting words, that Moshe would have to dance with his pain. Yet he did not feel like dancing.

In the weeks that followed, he had almost forgotten the man's strange advice, and when he sometimes remembered it, he dismissed it despite a vague anxiety.

When came that one night a year when it was the custom for the rebbe to dance in the synagogue of the yeshiva, Moshe was present with all the students, yet he felt that something forgotten, something important, was trying to reach him. He wanted to grasp it, but his attention was distracted by the rebbe, who rose to his feet unsteadily from the chair of honor, urged on by his students and the teachers. How would the rebbe ever be able to dance, to carry out his mitzvah? wondered Moshe – this year when the immaculately white-bearded figure seemed so ancient.

Slowly, one foot moving into place, the second following, the rebbe began to dance. His hands raised over his head, he turned slowly. Moshe thought briefly of Moses raising his hands to drive off Amalek. He felt it important that the rebbe hold up his hands. Moshe made a movement as if to help, then stopped himself. Perhaps the rebbe noticed for he approached Moshe, still dancing, and beckoned to him.

Moshe was dumbfounded and froze where he stood. The others divined the rebbe's will. "The rebbe wants you to dance," they urged him. "It is a great honor."

"Dance, Moshe," Yonah hissed.

Hesitantly, Moshe stood opposite the rebbe. The rebbe smiled and nodded.

Slowly, Moshe began to dance, hands held high. The students clapped their hands. Moshe forgot his self-consciousness. He danced with the rebbe, and as he danced, he felt the anxiety that still was part of him, the last remnant of doubt, weakening. Suddenly, he remembered the man's words and he was seized with a joy, the joy that comes to one secure in his faith. Moshe began to dance as if his life depended upon it.

Fishbein

Everyone in our family called the tuner of my daughter's piano "the piano tuner", though his name was Fishbein. He was a brusque man, even for a Viennese, stooped, often wore a checkered jacket which contrasted ridiculously with his formal striped pants, as if he had been a jazz saxophonist at one stage of his life and a concert pianist in another; his polka dotted, cabaret comedian's tie completed the total mismatch. He arrived, tuned the piano, refused tea and cake (not very Viennese), pleaded that he was late for another piano, grabbed his tuning case and hurried away. Always the same ritual. His statement about being late for another piano caused us to chuckle (after he left) because he spoke of the piano that awaited him like it was a person.

When he tuned the piano, he always tuned it to the same tune: the opening bars of "Pop Goes the Weasel,"which he tapped out with one finger, whose tip was blunted, seemingly from such use. This choice of his 'theme' amused us because my daughter's piano teacher insisted that she learn and practice classical music only, forbidding her to play "light," "frivolous" or "sentimental" music, the teacher's various descriptions with which she dismissed non-classical music. The piano tuner never requested my daughter to play anything for him, almost as if the piano interested him exclusively, its player superfluous.

The conversations between Fishbein and myself invariably led to his instructing me on the correct way to preserve his art; namely, how his tuning of the piano should be properly maintained. I would listen, nod, if scarcely paying attention. If the piano went out of tune, I reasoned, we would call him as usual. Once, fatigued of hearing the same lecture, and perhaps in ill temper by increasing worry over the way events were developing in Austria, I snapped that if we neglected our piano tuning preserving duties, he would profit by increased business. He vouchsafed me such a hurt look that

I was careful in the future to simply nod and say nothing.

Only once did the piano tuner and I have a conversation not connected to how the piano should be kept in tune. It took place sometime during the period before Hitler annexed Austria. Before Fishbein could begin his usual tuning lecture, I informed him that I didn't know how much longer we would need his services because we were going to flee Austria for Palestine. I urged him to do the same. Me? Palestine? Picking oranges? he asked. You can continue your profession of tuning pianos, I said, adding, that he was fortunate – his work did not require him to speak a new language. He shook his head slowly from side to side in negation of my suggestion. Vienna, he said, as if that explained all. Vienna is no longer Vienna, I answered. He nodded as if he agreed with this statement, said that he was late for another piano, and left.

We settled in Tel Aviv and gradually adapted to our new home. Sometimes, in the years that followed, when I heard someone playing the piano, I thought of the piano tuner back there -- who knew where he was, if he was, and sadness suffused me. After we arrived in Palestine, my daughter continued to study the piano for a time, although we couldn't afford to purchase a piano, practicing wherever a piano was available, but finally giving it up to became a translator to help us make ends meet. If the piano tuner had known about it, I thought, it would sadden him. Maybe even anger him. A luftmensch with his head in the clouds.

About a year ago, I was walking down Rabbi Berlin street, when I heard a tune being tapped out on the piano. The tune was familiar from somewhere, somewhere in the past. I stopped dead in my tracks. It was the opening bars of "Pop goes the Weasle." My body began to shiver. I ran to the door of the small, one-story house from which the music came and pressed frantically on the door bell. I kept pressing. The music stopped. A woman opened the door. I brushed past her. A man stood up – out of politeness, out of alarm? I ran to him, past a young girl. The woman's daughter learning the piano? The question flashed through my mind, albeit that my entire being was concentrated on the man who had stood up. Yes, it was Fishbein, older, face wrinkled, stooped even more, but it was he, wearing an open-necked white shirt and tan trousers. I spread my arms wide to embrace him. He was startled, although only momentarily, before falling as if in a faint into my arms. The mother and the girl, glimpsed from the corner of my eye, were staring at us open mouthed as if we were madmen. Tears flowed from my eyes. Tears flowed from Fishbein's eyes (perhaps this was Viennese also). He had heeded my advice.

There was indeed work for piano tuners outside of Vienna.

Eating Spaghetti with the Mafia

I was sitting at a table in a small Italian restaurant in the Sheepshead Bay area of Brooklyn. Being an insecure type, I sat with my back to the wall as usual when three nattily dressed gentlemen of Italian appearance entered and approached me. "This is our table. . ." the nattiest of them said to me softly and not impolitely. Maybe because of the gangster movies I had seen, or because of a sixth sense, I considered it best not to dispute the fact. If I were younger, I would have yielded with a humorous, face-saving remark, such as "I thought tables were fungible." If I were much younger, maybe even argued a bit, and perhaps I would have remained much younger for eternity. But fortunately I was not so young and life had taught me a certain prudence. "No problem," I said. "I'll sit somewhere else." I reached a hand toward a plate of spaghetti and meatballs that had arrived immediately before the three gentlemen – to take it to a table less in demand.

The ultra of the natty put forth a hand in my direction. Maybe my answer or ready compliance had struck a soft spot under the armor. "Wait a minute," he said. "You can join us." He seemed to have surprised his two brothers–in-possible-arms as much as me, for they glanced at each other momentarily.

I hesitated. These guys didn't seem out of Damon Runyon; I wasn't sure I wanted to be their dinner companion. "Thank you, but I don't want to disturb you," I said. "Probably you have business you want to discuss." "Business can wait," he said, glancing meaningfully (it seemed to me) at his two attendants whose body language seemed to relax at their being temporarily "off duty." He then turned to me once more. "Sit down," he ordered affably.

His subalterns looked me up and down. I had the feeling that they were searching me for under-my-clothes bulges denoting hidden weapons. I suddenly had the presentment that I was about to bend spaghetti elbows with three Mafiosos, one of them a don or whatever, and that rivals would burst into the restaurant "wasting" (I believe is the argot) the other guys at the table and not excluding me despite my comparatively poor dress. The odds were against such an occurrence, but I was at the stage of life where I already knew that things go against the odds more than one thinks. It was this latter conjecture that made me pause. But curiosity and a circumspect instinct not to protest too much decided me.

After I was seated, the leader sat down. The two subalterns sat down more slowly, after looking around the restaurant. This look-around I cherished (from the movies), I felt I was indeed present at a gangster meeting. The don looked disdainfully at my plate of regular spaghetti and meatballs. "You can do better. I'll order for you what I eat. You'll thank me later."

"What the hell," I thought. "Fine," is what I said.

He smiled a not unengaging smile, but not altogether reassuring. He waved his hand and there immediately appeared a heavy-set man whom I took to be the owner of the premises. (I had had a mere waiter.) His obvious interest in pleasing those who sat around me confirmed my suspicions as to the profession of my fellow diners. Only gangsters or media stars got such attention. And my three dinner partners didn't seem like media stars.

The ordering business was quickly completed, and

I noticed that the owner accorded me "star" treatment, too, even though I sat passively as the don ordered for me. Carried away by the moment, perhaps, I set my face to looking "hard" -- one of the gang – but feared I did not succeed. Although wanting desperately to look around the restaurant to bask in my celebrity company, I forbore, fearing, on one hand any sudden movement on my part and, on the other, getting "too cocky", "respect" reputedly occupying a near-mythic place in Mafia pantheon. Between mouthfuls of elaborately garnished spaghetti, the don was looking me over. I tried to ape his consummate ham-fisted fork and spoon spaghetti-lifting-and-devouring, but lacked his savoir-faire. I might have beaten him at knishes but we were on his turf.

I waited for him to begin the conversation. Maybe he liked to eat in silence.

I felt relieved when he began to exchange small talk with me.

(During the whole time the other two exchanged with me not a word. I sensed they were not overly happy with my being so chummy with the don. Or maybe "on duty," they were forbidden conversation. Maybe for the same reason, they didn't order. Or maybe they were dieting.)

At first, understandably, I was the passive dinner partner. He asked where I was from. "Trenton, New Jersey," I answered promptly. He owned he didn't know much about the place. Outside his turf, I speculated. "Between New York and Philly," I explained. He nodded, but I sensed he wasn't impressed. Somehow I thought it my duty to entertain him, that things would go easier that way. I groped for a subject. "Trenton was where 'Legs' Diamond hid out for a time." He looked interested. "In 'Hubby's Bar.'" I began telling the story of how on one occasion 'Legs' was hiding under the bar with a girl in a compromising position when the Feds (a term I thought he would like) came looking for him. The don chuckled and one of his bodyguards sniggered until the don gave him a half-look.

"You're not Italian" he said to me. I felt I had disappointed him. "No, my origins are from across the water, though." "The Mediterranean," I added lest he think I was referring to Jersey. "Jewish."

He nodded.

The conversation turned ethnic, but in a limited category. Italian and Jewish gangsters -- of the past. Maybe the 'Legs' Diamond gambit had provided an entry. Of course, the protagonists were never called "gangsters." We referred to them by name. He acknowledged that there were some good Jewish "boys" as he called them, having a special place in his heart for Lansky, whom he accoladed "smart." It soon became clear, however, that he thought the Italians superior in the field. I strove to bolster the Jewish position by reaching further back in history.

I brought out 'Two Gun Cohen,' so called because of the two pistols he wore as bodyguard for the Chinese political philosopher and first Chinese president, Sun Yat-Sen. Ok, so Cohen wasn't a gangster but a bodyguard, and not even a bodyguard of an underworld chieftain. And a Chinese philosopher might not stand big in the eyes of a guy whose philosophy, if from anywhere, came from the Borgias. Which is why I changed "philosopher and president" to "warlord." For good measure, I threw in some of the Odessa Jewish criminals from Babel's stories as well as Benia Krik, the Jewish bandit hero of Babel's eponymous novel. Ok again, so they weren't "wasters," merely thieves, but what can you do? I did not mention Shalom Aleichem's humorous offenders who obviously lacked clout. I racked my brains for Jews who had violated the worst of the Ten Commandments and preferably all ten.

The don was interested. "I never knew that," he

said more than once. On one occasion he turned to his two accessories, "Did you guys know that?" The body-guards shook their heads. We had finished the meal, including the wine the don had ordered and insisted I partake of, as well, a red wine we used to call "Dago Red" back in Trenton, which appellation I refrained from using on this occasion, although the Italians also used it. The wine had apparently gone to my head because I suddenly felt at home with the don.

"Delicious," I said (more than once, I'm afraid), and began to thank him for the experience. "Wait a minute," he said, leaning close to me, "you haven't had dessert." A voice inside me remembered the adage of an ancient Roman or modern gambler: 'You gotta know when to call it a day.' I begged off, patting my belly. "I'll get too fat."

"Nah," he said, "you gotta have dessert." It was an offer I couldn't refuse.

He ordered some small, furiously caloried cake. My panoply of Jewish gangsters exhausted, I began to tell some gangster jokes – at first utilizing Jewish names but, emboldened by his laughter, I began throwing in Italian names. He continued to laugh. The other two didn't laugh, although sometimes they couldn't restrain a smile.

He wiped a crumb from the corner of his mouth and stood up. The other two stood up. I quickly stood up. I expected the whole damn restaurant to stand up, and was surprised when they didn't. I felt a bit wobbly on my feet and hoped it wouldn't show.

The owner hastened with the bill – one bill and not two; he apparently knew his customer. "How much is my part?" I asked. "It's on me," the don said. I thought it best to accede. I thanked him overly, feeling relief that the meal had been completed successfully. He clapped me on the shoulder, "You ever need a favor, you let me know." The names of a few people who got on my nerves flitted through my thoughts, but I dismissed the idea.

I thanked him without pointing out that I didn't know his name. Maybe he thought everybody knew his name. Certainly everyone in the restaurant behaved as if they did.

He paused to say a few words to somebody at a table so that I exited ahead of the trio, unable, despite his generosity, to restrain the feeling that my back was vulnerable. I concentrated on avoiding a flinch.

I never learned who my host was. I was sorry later that I hadn't gone back to the restaurant to learn who he was. But prudence won out again. Maybe the don would have been insulted, or wondered why I was so interested. In that neighborhood the word got around fast.

The Fare

I turn to the passenger who has just entered my cab. When they enter like that without asking first, I know there won't be any quibbling over the price. No demand to put on the meter. "Where to?" I ask the salt and pepper-bearded man wearing an expensive suit and smartly made black brimmed hat, content that we can head off without negotiations.

"The next world."

A kibitzer. A surprise. The suit and hat had not prepared me for a kibitzer. And I am tired after a long day behind the wheel. "My license limits me to Jerusalem," I reply in a dry tone.

"Good – so long as it includes the Jerusalem on High."

" How about the central bus station? From there you can catch a bus to the next world."

"I suppose it's next best, if you can't take me."

Something in his tone tells me he isn't joking. I am used to conversations where I can bring my expertise to bear. The Betar Jerusalem football team, politics. But the next world, sorry.

My would-be passenger brightens. "Perhaps the cemetery? From there . . ."

There are cab drivers that refuse to take a fare to the cemetery. They are superstitious. I don't agree. I see it as a kind of mitzvah. And also I'm superstitious, but in the opposite direction. If you refuse all the time to take a fare to the cemetery, perhaps the Angel of Death will come to you and say: "So you stubbornly refused to go to the cemetery? Ok, I've come earlier than I planned to take you precisely there." But the usual fare is going to the cemetery to a funeral or to visit a grave – he doesn't plan to use it as a jumping-off point to the next world. No, I am not crazy about the idea of taking him to the cemetery. Maybe he's simply a weirdo. Then again, who knows?

"The cemetery is, ah, a bit far away. My work day is almost over." Then I add, already a bit piqued. "Why didn't you flag down a vehicle from the Burial Society?"

"You came along first."

"My luck," I mumble.

"Maybe you're right," he says, getting out of my cab. "I'll try the Burial Society. You have a Yiddishe kopf."

"I have a Kurdish kopf," I mentally reply, but only mentally. What I do say is: "Good luck." This is one fare I feel relieved to have lost.

He raises his hat to me in a quaint old European gesture of farewell. I prepare to pull away when I see in the mirror that he has flagged down a vehicle of the Burial Society! I see him speak to the driver. To my surprise, the driver does not pull away. Nor does the man enter to sit next to the driver, but goes around to the back of the vehicle, opens the door and enters.

I hit the gas pedal. I just want to get away. I am not curious to follow the vehicle to see what happens. I remember the tale of the four rabbis who went to Paradise. One went insane, and something bad happened to two others. Only Rabbi Akiba came back ok. I'm not Rabbi Akiba. I quickly turn right to get out of the vehicle's path. And into which street do I happen to turn? A street which has on its corner a building on which is written: "The Time Fixed for All Life": indicating that inside funeral orations are said prior to the burial ceremony. I'm sweating now. I keep going. The intercom comes to life. It's Rami. "What are you doing, Shuki?" he asks, angry. I can hardly tell him. "Stop wasting time," he shouts. "I need you right away."

"Go to hell," I tell him. I am immediately sorry. Not an expression for today. I quickly add, "Just kidding, Rami, what can I do for you?"

"A woman at 14 Zephaniah Street needs to get to the hospital on the double, she has birth pains."

More wonderful words, I have never heard Rami utter. A baby. Life. "The Lord be Praised!" I shout enthusiastically and push down on the accelerator.

Do I tell the other cab drivers my story? Of course not. They'll never believe me. Do I tell my wife? I don't know.

Would you?

The Manuscript

THE WINDOW WAS OPEN just enough to let in the cool night air. The finished manuscript lay on the desk, quiescent in the light from the full moon. It seemed to hint at some mystery beyond Kunzman's grasp. He thought of Bruno Schulz's story, 'The Book,' in which Schulz searches for The Book that contains the answers to everything, to the meaning of life, that he remembers from his childhood. He discovers the Polish maid tearing out its pages in order to wrap meat, and when he finally rescues it from her, all that remains are the advertisements at the back.

A feeling of panic seized Kunzman – that something similar might happen to his book. He had the sudden urge to get the book to the publisher before some disaster befell it. Being evening, the publisher was closed.

In bed that night, fearing a disaster to his manuscript, Kunzman slept with it near his bed, within arm's reach, waking from his fitful sleep from time to time to check on it. At one point he awoke, beads of sweat on his forehead, after dreaming that a critic dismissed his book with the Yiddish description, "bliyendike mistn" (manure in full bloom)." At another point he dreamt that he was Gregor Samsa who awoke one morning from uneasy dreams to find himself transformed into a gigantic insect who began to devour his book!

Awakening from this nightmare, he felt a two-fold sense of relief: that he had not been transformed into an insect and, almost as important, that he hadn't lost the book. He examined the book to make sure that none of the pages had been eaten.

Then a completely irrational thought assailed him: that he might die before he could deliver his book to the publisher. Timing his setting forth to bring him to the publisher precisely at the hour of opening, Kunzman carried the manuscript, feeling as if he held in his hands a sacred bird which would fly away if he relaxed his grip, declining to keep it under his shirt for safekeeping only because he feared he would look ridiculous.

The situs of the publisher was within walking

distance. And the whole way he feared some accident would befall the manuscript. Once handed over, Kunzman felt as if he had shed a great weight. An almost epiphanic joyfulness enveloped him. Yes, a time for celebration.

That night, unable to sleep, Kunzman imagined himself the alter ego to the young Dostoevsky after the latter delivered his first book, Poor Folk, to his editor. The editor had read it all night until, unable to restrain his enthusiasm for it any longer, he went to the author's residence, despite its being four o'clock in the morning, to inform him of his greatness. The next day he delivered the manuscript to a known literary critic and announced to him "a new Gogol is born!"

Crossroads

THE RAIN CONTINUED TO POUR, graying even more the stone of the monastery, the water seeping through the cracks and dripping into small pools on the stone floor. The wind swept around corners and under doors.

Brother Timothy entered the abbot's cell, holding his cowl tight at the neck in an effort to keep warm. Seeing the abbot's wan smile at his effort, he quickly released it.

The abbot tried to look grave. These young brothers feel guilty at every natural instinct of man, he mused.

"Yes?" he said in a voice devoid of all severity.

Brother Timothy shifted from his left foot to his right, then stopped, fearing the abbot might think he was trying to keep warm. The abbot realized that brother Timothy was ill at ease.

"There is ... whispering ..." the youth began awkwardly.

The abbot nodded and then said in a warm voice, "Continue, my son." He thought that brother Timothy deserved this expression of his warmth as recompense for his vouchsafement, however unsurprising the information. "Whispering is only a semi-violation of the vow of silence."

His irony went unrecognized.

"... whispering ... about you," brother Timothy added in a voice barely audible, looking around as if to ensure that no one overheard.

The abbot regretted having to spoil brother Timothy's good intentions. 'I know, my son."

The young monk's fingers played with the edge of his rough brown robe. "They say that you secretly study ... the Talmud."

The abbot sighed. He wanted to place his hand on brother Timothy's shoulder; to thank him for the risk he had taken upon himself, however unnecessary, since the abbot was aware that they knew. But beyond the fact that touching was an unacceptable act, brother Timothy could be at great risk if someone should see the abbot do so and conclude that brother Timothy was his disciple.

"My friend," said the abbot, using a personal reference rarely heard inside the gray walls. "I think it would be good for you to engage in good work among the poor for a time."

Brother Timothy could not conceal his surprise. "But I have never been outside these walls."

"It is time," the abbot said softly. "Believe me, to everything there is a time."

The Apartment Committee

The resident in Apartment 7 reflected that the apartment committee was a uniquely Israeli institution. He assumed that the socialist government which governed during the formative years of the State, in the days before the arrival of capitalism that threatened to divide the country into rich and poor, borrowed it from the then admired Soviet model, or perhaps it was a homespun concoction born of the model supplied by Yiddish Workman unions, or eagerly adopted from the "committee" approach so favored by the pre-State British Mandatory bureaucracy. He never troubled to investigate the matter, perhaps because he felt an antipathy toward the apartment committee due to his fear he would be drafted into serving on it. Each year when the time arrived for the apartment residents to appoint a new committee, he attended the meeting in trepidation. The reason he attended the meeting at all was to avoid being appointed to the committee in his absence, and only apprised of the fact the next day, faced with a fait accompli, a task from which he would be unable to extricate himself, or if so only after the most exhausting efforts, leaving him weak and enervated. Although he felt slight pangs of conscience about not doing his share, he assuaged his guilt by reminding himself that he always paid the committee-imposed resident dues on time, had never held back his payment because of some grudge against the committee for not acting on a request of his, and had always attended the committee meetings, one of the one-third of the apartment dwellers that, on average, bothered to do so.

He had in fact served on the committee once, unable to put it off after a number of years of avoidance, an experience that only served to deepen his vow to avoid serving again or at least to put it off as long as possible in the hope that the time would arrive in which the newer and younger apartment residents would take over – although as long as he could remember, the privilege seemed the prerogative of the middle-aged and above.

The committee had two responsibilities: one for maintenance, including that of the perennially problematic central heater, and one for finances, the collection of dues from the residents. Because of his lack of engineering and business acumen, when he served on the committee, he was given the financial duty. It was a headache. There were invariably those who refused to pay, claiming that the committee had committed this sin of commission or that sin of omission.

Madam Luka on the first floor was a regular offender. She spent a lot of money to redo her flat in a kind of Baroque-Spanish-Abbasid-motif, but was thrifty when the financial committee member came to her door in order to collect payments. She was numbered among those who believed in taking care of the family first, and only then paying her obligations to the rest of society, perhaps a harbinger of the capitalism that was to descend on the country in the mid-course of her long apartment tenure.

He, alas, belonged to the old school whose morality dictated payment, even if his family suffered financially as a result; in short, a product of the quondam socialist approach that had marked his formative years.

Then there was Branfman on the top floor, who dragged his heels in payment, demanding that the roof be re-tarred for winter so that his apartment would be less cold and damp. It goes without saying that he had never served on the committee. Branfman added insult to injury in that he would frame his complaints to the poor soul who came to collect dues in the form of interminable lectures, so that the collector would seek only to escape from him before his ears fell off. Small wonder that no one wanted Brandman on the committee! He was what is known as "a type," one that seems to come as part and parcel with every apartment building, as if mandated by a built-in clause in the builder's contract. Perhaps the good Lord created these types to keep us from being bored, he mused, or to allow cardiac specialists to make a living.

When someone refused to pay, it was a problem, particularly in the winter when the heat was shut off for lack of money to pay for fuel, and the rule was that unless everyone paid, no checks would be cashed. Usually a few days of Jerusalem cold was sufficient to induce payment, even by the most recalcitrant resident.

To his perpetual amazement, to the relief of the rest of the residents, there were those who agreed to serve on the committee for some years. As a result, the present committee had been in power for some time. Invariably, such long-time members constituted a sort of cabal who remained after the one-third of the residents who showed up for the committee meetings left. He was always happy to be the second to leave, as soon as someone else preceded him, relieved to not have been drafted to the committee, and eager to leave before someone suggested he should serve.

He was granted a reprieve with respect to the upcoming committee meeting, which was postponed for a week following the death of Shabtai in Apartment 12. Only the most cynical would contend that Shabtai, who was known as a wheeler-dealer, took this course of action to avoid serving on the committee.

Although he was bone-tired, the resident in Apartment 7 dragged himself off to the rescheduled committee meeting. Better tired now, than automatically committed in his absence.

As he descended to the bomb shelter in Entrance 2, where the meetings were held in the tomblike atmosphere of the windowless shelter, he tried to self-boost his spirits. The meeting, faithful to this history of its predecessors, got started late because it took time for the quorum to assemble.

The meeting began with some words of tribute to the late Shabtai by Cohen from Apartment 4 who was the dominant committee member and the only resident whose authority and mien demanded that he be addressed as "Mr. Cohen" and not by his first or last name. Cohen's imposing girth and heavy, dark beard caused the resident of Apartment 7 to muse that so must have looked the High Priest of the Temple of Old in Jerusalem, of whom, of course, the present Cohen was a descendant. Cohen's obituary reference to Shabtai was short, in deference to the mixed opinions of the residents about Shabtai, depending on their relationships, or lack thereof, built up over the years.

The resident of Apartment 7 half-listened to the mundane business at hand and only became tense when the subject of choosing a new committee was raised. Relief flooded him when the committee expressed its willingness to retain its present membership. Thus he was able to return to his apartment in high spirits, having been spared once again, Lazarus raised from the dead. His resurrection was cut short when he suddenly remembered that he would have to hurry to return to the site of the meeting in order to give back a key to the roof that he had borrowed to grant access the previous day to the repairers of his sun-heater. It couldn't wait for the next day, since Cohen was liable to rebuke him for the late return of the key. On the other hand, he feared going back lest his second coming somehow call forth the thought that he could be drafted onto the committee in place of one of them. He immediately consoled himself that it was Tuesday, the day of Creation twice "called good" – which augured well, that if he had escaped being drafted to the committee once on this day, he would perhaps escape it twice.

Thus emboldened, he hurried down to the shelter in order to catch Avram, a committee member, to return the key to him, avoid the severe Cohen, and slip out as quickly as possible. As he came to the door, he noted that it had been shut, which was odd. He hesitated whether to knock, and decided to put his ear to the door to hear whether the cabal was discussing something important or trivial; if the latter, he could interrupt them.

"It is time, gentlemen, to consider Gilad Shabtai's merits and lack thereof, in order to arrive at a decision," Cohen's voice intoned.

What kind of decision? He wondered, and how did Shabtai's merits or demerits concern the committee?

"We will begin, as usual, with his merits, since, as it is written . . ."

He couldn't catch Cohen's Biblical reference through the heavy door. There followed a recitation by each committee member of the merits of Shabtai, specific to time and place. He was astounded at their memories, or perhaps they were reading from notes. A detailing of a person's merits like that he'd never heard in his life. An eerie feeling overcame him. There was something heavy, serious, sepulchral in their recitations. As if they were deciding Shabtai's fate.

After a pause for some moments, they began to recite Shabtai's failings, once again specific to time and place. He strained to hear, his ear planted against the heavy metal door, having abandoned any attempt to interrupt them, yet unable to leave.

"The time has come to decide," he heard Cohen's voice. "Remember, Gilad Shabtai's place in the world to come is at stake: Paradise – or the Lower World. The Supreme Judge awaits our recommendation."

He couldn't believe his ears. Were they rehearsing a Purim spiel? But Purim was far away, and the voice of Cohen was more sober than he had ever heard it. And so were the voices of the rest of the committee members. They lowered their voices from time to time under the weight of their burden. He strained to catch each word.

He remembered that Shabtai had once supported him in his effort to have the committee pay for repair of a leaking pipe in his apartment. On the other hand, Shabtai had complained that he had shirked his responsibility to serve on the committee. But these were hardly the basis for deciding between Paradise or the Lower World.

Cohen's voice was louder now. "So it is decided –"

Cohen stopped speaking. At that moment, he, the avid listener, slipped on the perpetually damp floor of the stairwell and made a muffled sound.

"Wait," Cohen's voice had a different quality to it now, "I thought I heard someone outside . . ."

He froze, unable to move, then heard the sound of Cohen's footsteps coming closer. Girding his strength, he pushed himself upright and ran as silently as he could, his hair on end, up the stairs, encouraging himself that the sturdy Cohen was slow and walked with difficulty. The sound of the heavy door being opened slowly was followed by an eternal-seeming silence after which Cohen mumbled, "Nobody here," followed by the sound of the door being closed.

Ensconced in his kitchen, a cup of tea held with difficulty between his shaking hands, this time with brandy added, the resident of Apartment 7 mulled over what had happened. Could he have really heard what he had heard? He couldn't have – and yet he remembered that on more than one occasion a committee meeting had shortly followed the death of an apartment resident. Perhaps his efforts to remain off the committee were not as transparent as he had thought. In a way, he felt insulted; apparently they did not consider him worthy of more important matters than knocking on the residents' doors to collect committee dues.

On the other hand, maybe one had to apprentice on the committee's more mundane tasks before being granted permission to decide more weighty ones. Maybe one was even required to serve more than one term (and not grudgingly) over a period of many years.

He suspected he would continue to avoid serving on the committee; the responsibility was too much. He had made a parallel decision, however: he would attend synagogue on a more regular basis. Shabtai, he remembered, had over the years become something of a slacker.

Like a Candle

THE OTHER DAY I RAN INTO MISCHA of the famous trio from the days of the satiric theater The Kettle — "Mischa, Mendel and Moris", whose shtick " See No Evil, Hear No Evil, Do No Evil" was the big hit that left all Tel-Aviv rolling in the aisles with Mischa in the role "See No Evil." By the way, Moris was the stage name of Beryl Pomerantz. Mischa and Mendel used their real monikers. Mischa was apparently in a nostalgic frame of mind because he greeted me enthusiastically, putting his arm around me. We exchanged information on how each other was (holding our own), and what was new (not much). There followed a silence in which neither of us apparently had anything more to say. Suddenly Mischa brightened. "You want to see where Mendel and Beryl and I lived during our early days when we appeared at the kettle and afterwards?" I didn't, but though he put it to me as a question, I knew, with a sinking feeling, that it was an offer I couldn't refuse, not if I didn't want to alienate him for life. I was at an age where I didn't want to alienate anyone for life, since so many of my former cronies were no longer in life. Nor those of Mischa – in particular, Beryl and Mendel. So I agreed to Mischa's offer despite my rule: don't look to the past, look to the future. But, as I said, I could see it was important to Mischa, who, after all, had done me some favors, one of which had a significant effect on my life (ok, he introduced me to my wife).

He took me to an old neighborhood on the border of Little Tel-Aviv, where the timeworn buildings were losing their battle against modernity. We entered one of them. Mischa was chummy with the superintendent – Boris in "Bella and Boris", who nobody remembers anymore, except Mischa and of course, Boris. (Bella passed away after Alzheimer's and she didn't remember Boris at the end.)

Mischa accompanied us to the apartment, a large room with a bathroom and kitchen. Now it was uninhabited and served as a store-room. Mischa turned the rusting key, let us in and left us alone with our memories, or rather Mischa's. Bits of old furniture and junk here and there. "Nothing much from our day, 'cept the lamps," Mischa mumbled.

The place made me uncomfortable. Dingy was the word for it. I don't like old things.

Mischa stood there, silent, either uncomfortable, too, or going back over some memories connected to the place. I stood there respectfully, my mind blank, waiting until he had seen enough. I debated with myself whether a decent amount of time had passed to enable me to thank him for the visit as a means of putting an end to it. I didn't get the chance because Mischa snapped out of his thoughts, looking around the place once more. Maybe he discerned that I felt uncomfortable, maybe he simply had fulfilled his purpose, because he turned as if to leave, then stopped. "Let's each take a bulb from the lamps, for the memory, for old times' sake," he said.

I didn't care for the idea, but I could see it was important to him. He began to carefully unscrew one bulb. I feared it would crumble from age, but it didn't. Maybe they made them tougher in those days. Mischa looked up from his unscrewing and nodded to me to begin. I did so. Suddenly tears are running down his cheeks. Tears began to run down mine.

I put the bulb carefully into my pocket. On the way home, I couldn't bring myself to throw it away. I felt like to do it would be to murder something. Maybe Mischa. Maybe Mischa, Mendel and Moris. I put it in the oldest lamp I had that would still take a bulb like that, and used it until it burned out.

Like a candle, I thought. Like a candle to their memories.

Lebanon

He found it strange to find himself a panda trying to maneuver in a man-made machine. The machine is a jeep. Under layers of various protective clothing topped by a flak-vest, grasping the butt of a machine gun, wedged between gun, seat, sides of the jeep, the radio and various moveable chattels. He sits facing rearward. Such a position is also metaphysical (as he moves, does he not view the past?), and one sharpened by exposure to putative danger: it is Lebanon. Is this real?

Escort duty. Up into the mountains. He places the ribbon of bullets within the silvery clasp of the gun. The air is crisp and clean. In some places, copses of long-trunked trees with curious tufts on top which, with the mossy-appearing grass-covered hills surrounding them, give the landscape a Chinese aspect.

Even the golden-tipped machine gun bullets shine in the sun like small golden-roofed pagodas. Perhaps it is appropriate: twenty-four centuries before, Chuang Tzu dreamt he was a butterfly and did not know when he awoke, if he was a man who had dreamt he was a butterfly or a butterfly who now dreamt he was a man.

Sometimes he is asked – when joined by other than his usual jeep's crew – if he "knows how to shoot." It gives him a certain pride to reply in the affirmative. The words confirm a certain power similar to, but even greater than, that felt when he helped clean and oil the guns, their lubricated metallic parts moving smoothly into place, a sense of mastery-over-machine. Even putting the ribbon of bullets into its silvery holder and slamming its cover shut has a neat feel to it, like a knight-errant slamming shut his visor. One is a professional – even at forty-six, balding, often tired, sometimes rained on – yet momentarily one of the Magnificent Seven.

Momentarily. After some days bracing himself within the jeep and bouncing at bumps the Lebanese roads so thoughtfully provide, he begins to feel it in the legs like an aging boxer. How old was Chuang Tzu when he dreamt he was a butterfly?

He might have dreamt he was a mouse, like the one who peeps over the roof vent of their tent with small inquisitive, perhaps Chinese eyes; his scurrying over the roof becomes a pleasant, comforting sound. Sounds and sights accrete in Lebanon: gray clouds dwarfing an El Greco Toledo; the dominating presence of Beaufort Castle from its height on the cliffs; silver and green olive trees; mountains with rocky sides scarified as if with ancient writing. The code names sputtering over the jeep's radio: "nightingale, nightingale." Also Chinese.

Snow falls. The hills, not just the mountains, covered with white, villages huddled against their flanks. He huddles against the sides of the jeep, jamming the butt of the machine gun against his shoulder, pinioned between it and the seat to be less a rolling target for the elements, like a crow's-nest-lashed watch in a nineteenth century whaler. Up into the hills, deeper snow, the jeep crossing rivulets where the muddy brown flow gathers at points in the road, making waves. From the hills, the jeep must appear a beetle crawling across the snow. Perhaps he is the beetle, or the beetle is Chuang Tzu. Or Chuang Tzu is he.

The Man Who Ate at Funerals

YOU WILL SAY THAT I LIVE OFF THE DEAD. That's what somebody said I did. He was right, in a sense. I do it for sustenance. You have to live, right? I use my meager pension for medicine and other needs. Food I have taken care of by living off ... When my wife was alive, we managed, but when it came to food once I was alone, I couldn't. Until I stumbled on the idea.

It came to me when I read that the Polish writer Witold Gomobrowicz, trapped in Argentina when the Second World War broke out, because of his lack of income attended funerals in order to help himself to food afterward at the mourners' meals. If it worked for Gomobrowicz, I reasoned, why not for Pearlman?

"It is better to go to the house of mourning, than to go to the house of feasting," says Ecclesiastes. I tried to combine the two. If I saw a funeral notice in the newspaper or on the death notices pasted on billboards or building entrances, I would copy down the address. True, I had to know something in order to explain my relationship to the deceased, so I came to the meal where they sat shiva after the funeral, or I went to the funeral and caught a ride from a mourner at the funeral. This latter method required more effort, but it established my credentials better than when I simply showed up for the meal.

While still new at the business, I would say that while I didn't know the deceased well, after we passed each other on the street a number of times, there developed a kind of friendship between us. At first, we exchanged greetings, and then a few words in passing, and sometimes stood and talked a bit. While we weren't close friends, I wanted to honor the deceased's memory. My explanation proved to be sufficient. What might have been considered odd from a younger person was acceptable from an elderly one.

Later I perfected my technique. I learned from the newspaper obituaries in the library, or what I overheard before or after the funeral when the mourners exchanged memories of the deceased or otherwise presented their credentials as mourners. Here the temptation was to exaggerate my knowledge of the deceased based on such information, but I restrained myself , and no one questioned me. The atmosphere did not encourage investigation. I further resisted the temptation to deliver a eulogy based upon my researches.

When the deceased was a woman, I had to dispel any suspicion that I may have been her lover. My wearing sunglasses because my eyes had become weaker may have convinced them I sought anonymity. In addition, I was always a debonair dresser, even if my suits are somewhat threadbare. I felt like an impoverished Spanish grandee in this respect: poor but proud. Though the idea amused me to play the ex-lover, it was too risky.

In the beginning of my culinary career, so to speak, all my strategy was bent on obtaining a free meal. But later I became more interested in the deceased per se because of my "researches." It lessened the boredom of my life. I got tired of waiting for the day to become night and the night to become day, the feeling that I was already living a posthumous existence, nisht ahien, nisht aher – "neither here nor there." I listened to and even took part with the mourners at reminiscing about the deceased. In some cases I came to almost believe I had known him or her. Perhaps the feeling of "belonging" became as important as the meal itself. "Food for thought," I told myself.

And then it happened. Perhaps it was bound to happen. The Yiddish saying, 'Two people can keep a secret if one of them is dead' doesn't always apply. When I read about the deceased in question, there was something familiar about him, yet I couldn't place what it was. At the meal, I gradually remembered, based on the conversation around me that I had known the man many years before. Suddenly one man pointed a finger at me and shouted, "I remember you! Jacob told me how you blocked his promotion because you believed you deserved it yourself."

It was true -- I recalled it before my accuser had finished his sentence. Later my conscience had troubled me about it. Now I tried to explain. "I was young and ambitious. I regretted it later." All eyes were upon me. The deceased's sister turned on me, "How dare you come here!" For once at a loss for words among the mourners, beginning to sweat, I looked for a way to exit as gracefully as possible. "I felt guilty – that's why I came," I stammered, sounding unconvincing even to my own ear. There was a silence, a hostile silence. I stood, mumbled something about having to leave, uttered quickly the words of traditional comfort, and exited rapidly, before things could turn ugly. The words of the prayer recited after the meal pursued me: "That he will not be ashamed in this world and a disgrace in the next ."

If a person died who was close to my age, I felt uncomfortable, too close a reminder that someday the funeral would be mine. I wondered if someone would come to my funeral in order to scrounge a meal. I couldn't decide if the thought bothered or amused me. Probably the fare wouldn't be anything to brag about, given my relationship with the mishpocheh (relatives). I toyed with the idea of putting a provision in my will to cover the cost of the meal, even if it might prove unenforceable for lack of funds.

Sometimes it was possible to introduce humor, or irony, if the funeral was not a tragic one for someone who died before his time. (I avoided going to tragic funerals – I would not feel comfortable "stealing" a meal, and the atmosphere is too oppressive.) Humor: 'the oil of joy for mourning', if you like. Used to containing my pain, I now had to produce pleasure. Not so easy.

Once when someone mentioned the last words of the deceased, I told them the last words of Oscar Wilde, "This wallpaper is killing me; one of us has got to go," and though they didn't know who Oscar Wilde was, they laughed. And I felt I had "earned" my meal and was not merely a schnorrer, that I had freed myself from the Yiddish admonition, a nemer is nit kayne gever – "one who takes doesn't give." Just as there was a wedding badhan, a professional jester who traditionally entertained guests at a marriage feast, I fancied myself a mourning badhan, something that had never existed before. Sometimes, if the mood was light and the subject of gravestone inscriptions came up, I told them what Frank Sinatra (they knew who he was) had had inscribed on his gravestone: 'The best is yet to come.'

If I wanted to introduce humor at a Sephardic funeral, the humor had to be at the expense of someone. The Ashkenazim are the opposite—they target themselves, perhaps a product of the insular shtetl. For the Ashkenazim, honor was not important. Love, maybe? Bialik said, 'They say there is love in the world. What is love?' Love was Bella. That's why I didn't marry again. I feared I would forget Bella. The new bride would confuse or dilute my memory of Bella. At my age holding on to memory is difficult enough.

I'm not so sure Sinatra had it right, yet I try to remain optimistic. The medieval rabbis saw heaven as a vast, quiet, peaceful library, where books jumped down from the shelves when you nodded to them, and soft-footed librarians dispensed cooling mint drinks. Ok, maybe with a bit of schnapps.

I appreciate the positive face Judaism puts on toward the next world. 'May his soul be gathered in eternal life.' is inscribed on gravestones. The next world is called 'the world of the living.' In the Temple in Jerusalem the Levites sang on the seventh day, 'Sing a song for the Sabbath. Sing a song to the future to come, to the day that all of it is the Sabbath and rest for eternal life.'

Halevai. Would that it be so.

Once, under the influence of two many cognacs, I disclosed my means of sustenance to a fellow imbiber. "You live off the dead," he said. And then he added, soberly, "You can atone by volunteering to 'purify the dead.'" He meant that I should carry out the mitzvah of washing the deceased before burial. Although I recoiled from the suggestion, the idea of late gnaws at me. Live off the dead—purify the dead. More than symmetry, a settling of accounts.

A Piece of String

One evening, going through the work of my ex-boss, the late literary critic, Saul Lieberman, I came across a piece of string. The find touched my heart: I remembered that Lieberman loved to fondle a piece of string while he wrote, or to wrap it around his finger

One Hanukah, someone sent Lieberman, anonymously, a present of a string of Arab worry beads of the kind ubiquitously found in the Old City. There was no need for the donor to enclose a note instructing that the gift be used in lieu of Lieberman's string. Lieberman spent a week trying to find out who had sent it before giving up. It could have been any of the staff. Unable to pin the blame individually, he contented himself with a sweeping condemnation of the staff. "It is preferable to be a lion at the head of an army of mice than the opposite," he grumbled. Me,

Lieberman had eliminated as a subject at once. "Not your style," he said. I didn't know whether to take this as praise or condemnation.

For some days after I found it, I couldn't get "Lieberman's string" out of my head. I had put it in my pocket, undecided whether to bring it to the attention of his widow, Victoria. A few days after, when I went to her place to work further on her late husband's unfinished book, I took it with me. Victoria received me sitting in the padmasana position. "I could never sit in that pretzel position," I confessed to her. "I'm not surprised," she replied. I was about to get back at her by asking if Lieberman could – but decided it wasn't a good idea to begin a visit with Victoria on the wrong foot. Moreover, the string in my pocket demanded attention. Deciding to show it to Victoria, I explained where I had found it.

Victoria disentangled herself from the lotus position to stand leaning against the book-case. "Lieberman clung to string like a child to a blanket," she said in a neutral tone, neither affectionately nor critically.

"Perhaps you would like to keep it", I said. "To remind you …"

"No," she said in what to me sounded to me, oddly, as a frightened tone. After a pause, "I do not like physical reminders of … You keep it."

I put it in my pocket. The truth is that I wasn't crazy about keeping it either; on the other hand, it seemed a sacrilege to discard it.

Some days later, working on the book, I inserted the string between a sheaf of pages of Lieberman's material, returning it to its "resting place." Yet the string refused to leave me, surfacing in my mind from time to time.

Alas my romantic relationship to Victoria was destined to come to an end when the book did. A month after the book was published, Victoria told me that the relationship was over. "All things come to an end, Kunzman," she added, trying to soften the blow.

Victoria may have considered it a gentle dismissal, and perhaps it was, but it was anything but gentle for me.

"I had hoped . . ." I protested.

Victoria was wearing culottes. I hated culottes. Did she know this? Did she wear them today on purpose?

She stood feet wide apart like some female Colossus. She put her beautifully-shaped finger on my lips. "Don't say anything," she said.

"But . . ." I persisted huskily, feeling like the shriveled, dwarfish man so often portrayed in drawings by Bruno Schulz, face twisted with yearning, crawling toward the foot of a woman who is majestic in her indifference to him.

The night of the day that Victoria 'dismissed' me I spent walking and ruminating, ruminating and walking. I continued to walk, oblivious of my surroundings (I vaguely sensed I passed through the dark and abandoned alleys of the German quarter), my thoughts consuming me. The hours followed each other. It began to rain. Victoria did not like rain. I did. The rain was not strong, and the drops felt mild and somehow welcome. Did I hope that someday Victoria would return to me? Not really, I had no illusions on that score – and yet what?

To paraphrase an imp in a story of I. B. Singer: In Paradise even the wise are the footstools of the beautiful. Lieberman, I recalled, disliked romantic novels. And if I had triumphed over Lieberman, so to speak, in having enjoyed his wife (however manipulatively on her part), Lieberman had triumphed over me posthumously, as he had in life, by getting his book published – a book largely written by Kunzman, the loser. And I knew that one of these days I would see Victoria arm-in-arm with another man; I wouldn't know if she loved the new man or was using him as she had used me. Surely, seeing the man, I would think, "Et tu, Brutus." And from somewhere would come the echo, "Tut, tut, Kunzman." In the voice of Lieberman, of course.

Greenfield Stands Alone

THE GREAT JEWISH MYSTICS were influenced by their environment. And it is no less so with their spiritual descendants, of whom one was Jacob Greenfield, center fielder, although he would never characterize himself as being a member of that sublime group. Broiled under an August sun that causes the faces of the few fans present to shimmer in the heated air like disembodied heads, or frozen in the hail and frost of an April in a year when winter refuses to accommodate to the cry "Play ball", ankle deep in mud amidst a monsoon which an umpire refuses to recognize as nothing but a summer shower – in such times of adversity Greenfield's soul was shaped.

Yet it is the hazards caused by their fellow-man that proved most searing to the mystics' soul. In this, Greenfield was no different. The victim of showers of popcorn, peanut shells and other missiles from opposing fans, he stood them all. Yes, these and more Greenfield braved in times of non-action.

Like his spiritual forebears, Greenfield's life was not less tested in times of action. He was forced to judge how a ball will ricochet off a particular wall -- with a web of possible ricochets depending on the substance and angle of the wall in each stadium. The need to concentrate on the descent of a sphere out of a burning sun while ten thousand grouped in the center field stands scream for you to drop the ball -- in such times men are made. So it was with Greenfield. And in the despair when the ball is dropped, or misjudged, so that it falls to earth untouched by one's glove, and in the hoots of a capricious mob that fall upon one's ears – a forging of the soul is bred.

And then there are the times of loneliness, when the stands are empty or almost so, and the center fielder's only company is the wintry blast of the wind when the shadows have fallen across his position like dimming hope upon the shades of the Underworld. It is in these times, when the effectiveness of a pitcher keeps the action -- the unfolding of events seemingly a thousand miles away – subdued: the strike-outs, the dribbling balls to the infield, that the center fielder has time for reflection. In these times he comes into his own. For most of the breed, perhaps, this time is less well used – concentrated in the mechanical action of jaws upon gum, or upon tobacco, or thinking of girls and things not of the spirit. But such squandering of precious moments was not for Greenfield.

In these intervals of reflection, Greenfield's mind expanded beyond the confines of the stadium and became one with the cosmic world that lay beyond it. He thought of the sefirot, the ten attributes/emenations in Kabbalah through which the Infinite reveals itself and continuously creates the physical and the chain of higher metaphysical realms. And especially, the sefirah Teferet that represents the ideal balance of Justice and Mercy needed for the proper running of the universe. In such moments, a careful observer might notice a detached, and sometimes a radiant, expression upon Greenfield's burnished visage. His brethren in the out-field, Grady at left and Benson at right, lacked similar aspirations. They did what was required of them, no more; actions which Greenfield copied only when demanded by the game: a word of encouragement in a difficult situation, leisurely throwing the ball after a put-out – such were carried out with appropriate, detached, participation on his part.

Aside from such obligations, he was free. In these solitary moments, his philosophy was formed. Greenfield did not articulate it as such, couldn't be expected to. His philosophy was forged in his small moments of vexation, as in his great ones of triumph. The latter – the gunning down of a runner at the plate on a perfect throw, for instance, whereby arc and angle and velocity synergized – perhaps contributed less than the failures: the dropped balls and kindred befallings. Greenfield was molded by everything he experienced within that crucible bounded by the wall and the respective territories of the right and left fielders. Yet he was the center fielder, whose very name pointed to the mystic center for Greenfield, the Kabbalistic point of the universe around which existence and world revolved.

He was exposed, a point on a sea of grass, between the Scylla of hostile fans and the Charybdis of hostile elements of nature. Armed only with the skin of a cow on one hand which stung when the sphere smashed it as he pinioned his body high against a wall no less hard than that which surrounded Jericho, any beauteous Rachel who appeared close to him when he approached the centerfield stands, and smiled down at him – he could never meet. Nor could he shout out his desire for her where his feeling would be hooted at by the unfeeling mob, or worse – a thousand times worse – imitated: "I want you" howled in derision and reverberating throughout the stadium like the clash of hostile blades upon iron shields. No, they would never meet: a fleeting exchange of appealing looks – a moment in time, a mutuality of evanescence – was all he had as keepsake. These things, too, molded Greenfield – sometimes he would see her face (if it was still her face or only the giving of form to hope in his mind), often at the loneliest times – in locker rooms where other maidens from the pages of sex magazines looked out, mocking, mocking.

If day presented such challenges, the night 'games' multiplied them. Blinding lights coming out of a sea of darkness, the crowds' faces garish like skulls in the glare, the softness of day banished, and the sounds of the night crowds metallic, like the beating of tin drums. Unlike day games, night games could produce dark terrors in a sensitive soul like Greenfield, causing him to feel less a son of Samson than a Roman gladiator set before the mob. Yet they, too, contributed to his philosophy, gave it its patches of darkness.

In the end, however, it was time that came to be the principal ingredient of Greenfield's philosophy.

For what was the game in which he participated but a marking of time. Not in the crass sense of other sports routinely set against the clock. The game he participated in measured time – the leisured intervals between plays, the slow movement of time set against the rapidity of time – meted out in seconds – of the game itself: the movement of ball to bat, to field, and the runner's counterpointed movement. Time and movement. Set upon a measured field of base paths and distances to walls. No wonder the game so fascinated Greenfield. For time was dissected: fast, slow, slow, fast, and all the times in between. The game had a rhythm, but an unpredictable rhythm in which his own movements and measurings had their rightful place. When this discovery came to Greenfield, he marveled at it. So simple it was, and yet so portentous.

As a result, there grew gradually in his subconscious and upward to his consciousness the awareness that he was upsetting the universal rhythm. That he was aging. That his days were numbered and that younger men waited to stand in his place at the mystic center. It became obvious to everyone – especially to Greenfield himself – that he was no longer getting the jump on the ball, that more and more of the spheres were falling to the ground, or eluding his glove which did not quite reach the place it should be at in time. And Greenfeild was aware of something else: he was overcompensating – trying too hard to position himself so that he would have to run less, relying on too precise an attempted estimation of where the ball would land, instead of relying on the previously automatic knowledge contained in his boundless self. In short, his freedom was gone. His time had changed – the easy rhythm was lost.

After a day in which he dropped two flies, and the wind flagged his shirt in playful taunts, Greenfield walked out of the stadium into its shadows, handed his glove to a small boy who accepted it wide-eyed, and walked peacefully, almost happily, to the river beyond the stadium he had felt running under his feet, under the center field turf, and stared at it, as if it were the river Gihon in the Garden of Eden. And he felt uplifted, for does not "Eden" mean "bliss" or "joy"?

Invention of the Beygl

KUNI FREMEL SAT STARING AT HIS PLATE OF LOX and cream-cheese in the shtetl of a small Polish village of unpronounceable name not far from its more impressive neighbor, Chelm.

"It's not going to leap into your mouth," his wife Farfela told him.

"I know, crown of my life. But for some time now every time I sit down to a repast of lox and cream-cheese, I feel that there is something missing."

Farfela folded her arms. "And what might that be?"

"I don't know, raisin and almond for life. I just don't know."

It got to the point where Kuni couldn't put a bite of lox, or cream-cheese, in his mouth. "Something is missing" an inner voice told him. "I know, I know

– but what?" he would ask out loud, so that soon the whole village was whispering about him.

One night he had a dream. Lox and cream-cheese danced before his eyes, hand in hand with – something round like Ezekiel's wheel.

Kuni leapt out from his bed, carefully, so as not to wake Farfela, and tip-toed to the kitchen.

The next morning Farfela was surprised to see the remains of a lox and cream-cheese meal. She confronted Kuni. "You ate it – the lox and cream-cheese. Don't try to deny it!"

"Who's denying, precious spice of my life. I discovered what was missing – the roll." He brought a kind of hard roll from the oven. "Taste that."

"Not bad, but too heavy," she commented.

In his heart of hearts, Kuni knew Farfela's judgment was sound. "Too heavy," he shook his head sadly.

For days he experimented with his roll, until one day, in the month of Kislav, he chanced to see a full moon surrounded by a cloud circle. A message from Heaven. He ran to the kitchen and prepared his center-holed creation.

"Taste this, ornament of my days," he proffered to Farfela.

"Not bad, not bad," she agreed. "And it makes a good place on which to spread the cream-cheese."

"You are right, of course, spicemeat of my nights."

"Now, don't get carried away," she admonished him. But who could blame him? He had invented the beygl , from the Middle High German 'böugel' or ring.

Uncle Lepke

ONE DAY, WHEN I WAS SIX OR SEVEN, I lost the doorkey to our house, as we called our tenement apartment. Every day after school I would let myself in and eat the meal mom left for me on the dining room table and keep myself busy, in her words, till she got back from work at six.

For a quarter of an hour after school that day, I looked for the key in the playground where I assumed I'd lost it. I concentrated on the area under the monkey bars where I would hang upside down for minutes if the other kids weren't clamoring for their turn. I liked to think in that position (convinced the blood running to my head spurred ruminating), a practice that earned me the nickname "sloth" among some of the kids and "monkey" among others. Even a blow once in a while from Flanagan who didn't like me and looked for an excuse to give me a fist in "the kishkes" while I hung, though I usually avoided it, since my thinking didn't prevent me from seeing him approach, and when he tried to come at me from behind, a sixth sense (and his heavy tread) alerted me. I don't know whether the hanging bothered him or the thinking (Flanagan wasn't a great thinker) which, as I said, I liked to do in that position. Later I heard he was killed in the war which left me with mixed feelings.

After not finding the key, I was depressed because of the long afternoon I would have to spend hungry and possibly in need of going to the bathroom -- I abhorred public toilets, abnormally fearful of 'germs' at that age, and the faucet to wash my hands often didn't work and I worried that the germs would reach every part of my body before mother would let me in and I could wash my hands. But I was even more depressed at the thought of her being angry at me because I lost the key.

I sat on the curb after school, chin in hands, and thought. And then I remembered my uncle, Louis Buchalter, lived on the way home from school. He was known in the neighborhood as "Lepkeleh" – "Little Louis" in Yiddish to some (that's what his mother called him), and "Lepke" to others less well-disposed toward him. My mother said that he wasn't really an uncle but a more distant relative. I think maybe she said this because of his reputation. "A nogoodnik" she sometimes called him on the rare occasions when rumors, or, more frequently, the newspapers, linked him to some murder. A relative once observed that I looked somewhat like him, and from that day my mother put her on her blacklist of relatives not to be invited to family events. I was rather pleased by the supposed resemblence. Once, at a Thanksgiving meal with relatives, cousin Marvin said that Lepke and his "cronies" had killed a lot of people. Aunt Gertrude shushed him, looking at me pointedly. When Uncle Lepke sent my mother 500 dollars for my brother's bar mitzvah, she sent it back, explaining to us that the money was "tainted". 500 smackers! A sum my mother worked half a year to earn.

At night sometimes I pleasurably scared myself with thoughts of Uncle Lepke's killing someone. I imagined gunshots, knives, running over by cars, and worse. Later I learned I wasn't far off the mark. And yet when I lost my key, I feared my mother more than I feared Uncle Lepke, maybe because in the back of my mind being his relative gave me protection. And so I decided to go to his place and ask if I could stay there till quarter to six, and then I would go home, without mentioning to my mother, of course, where I had been. I would tell her I hung around in the park or visited a friend. I was an inventive kid.

So I went to Uncle Lepke's building – all the kids knew where he lived. I would usually detour around the site, or if in a hurry run on the other side of the street, my bedtime imaginings of his murders out-weighing whatever protection I thought being his relative afforded. But that was before I lost the key. The more daring kids walked slowly by "Lepke's"; in my opinion they were just the types to go into the same business, maybe in slowly passing his building they hoped to 'be discovered'.

On that day I didn't detour or run by, but slowly mounted the steps to the building. I looked furtively inside to see if there was a guard toting a tommy-gun, but I saw no one. I thought for a moment I had the wrong place, but checking the names of the build-ing residents, I saw his – printed the same size as the others, a disappointment to me, though looking back I considered it a nice touch. The guard was further inside, I assumed, or standing, legs wide apart, tommy at the ready, outside Uncle Lepke's door.

Uncle Lepke lived on the third floor. For some reason I feared the steps would creak (as often happened in the scary radio program The Shadow, ("Who knows what evil lurks in the hearts of men?"), but they didn't. The guard was sitting outside the door on a simple wooden chair. No tommy-gun, yet the bulge under his natty jacket told me he wasn't a doorman. Seeing me head toward the door, he stiffened momentarily, but my age or innocent features must have put him at ease. Maybe he thought I had the wrong address. "Yeah, sonny?" he addressed me. Was he Lepke's partner, Albert 'Mad Hatter" Anastasia?

"I'm looking for Mr. Buchalter," I stammered.

His right eyebrow went up at this."Whattaya want with him?" His hand didn't reach for a gun, but his tone wasn't friendly.

"He's my uncle," I said quickly.

"Really?" was all he said. He looked me over. Maybe he's checking for resemblance, I thought.

"Really," I answered, sort of proud despite the thought that my mother would disapprove. "I lost my key and thought that maybe I could stay with Lep – Mr. Buchalter until my mother returned home from work."

For some moments which seemed to me an

eternity he didn't say anything, merely chewed his gum slowly. Then he stood up. "Stay here," he ordered, and went inside. I didn't sit on his chair. Maybe he wouldn't like it. Maybe I might be mistaken for the guard by a hitman from a rival gang who chose that moment to settle a beef with Buchalter.

A short time later he returned and patted me on the head. "The boss will see you," he said, pointing to the door. Maybe he was one of Lepke's hitmen – Abe 'Kid Twist' Reles, Seymour 'Blue Jaw' Magoon, Frank 'Dasher" Abbandando, Harry 'Happy' Maione, Albert 'Tick-Tock' Tannenbaum or Harry 'Pittsburgh Phil' Strauss, whose names we kids knew almost as well as we knew the names of famous baseball players. I wondered if Uncle Lepke saved money by using his hitmen also as guards. Maybe that's how he could afford 500 dollar bar mitzvah gifts, a lot more expensive than the traditional fountain-pen.

I entered. The hitman remained outside. As soon as I stepped in, another hitman gestured to me to follow him. We left the hallway and entered a room where a man in a dark blue suit with deep set eyes and a determined mouth awaited me. To my disappointment I didn't see any trace of resemblance to me in his face. He was nattier dressed than the hitman.

What caught my eye was the point of an immaculately pressed white handkerchief jutting out of the breast pocket of his suit jacket. I wondered if it had been steam-pressed at Drezner's Dry Cleaners. Maybe with all 'the help' Uncle Lepke didn't have to dirty his hands.

I quickly surveyed the room, wanting to remember it to tell my brother and maybe some of my closest friends who could keep a secret. A dapper fedora hung on an antler of a hat stand. On the wall a photograph of Al Jolson in blackface, on his knees, his white-gloved hands spread wide apart, his mouth wide open, the finale to one of his songs, maybe 'Mammy.' The picture disturbed me – without being able to hear the song it looked like Al was begging for his life. From Uncle Lepke.

"So you're my little relative," he said. His voice was lighter than I expected. His smile (I was amazed he smiled at all) more winning than I would have imagined.

"Yes, my mother Rose is your ..." I hesitated " . .. relative."

"Ah, Rose," a pretty name." I wasn't sure he remembered Rose as a relative. "So you lost your key and need a pad."

The hitman must have told him. I felt embarrassed

that I lost the key, something I was sure he would never do. "Yes, sir, on the monkey bars in the school playground, I think. I was hanging upside down and it must have fallen out."

"Yeah," he chuckled, "hanging isn't a good idea. You can stay here. And you can eat something, too. You could do with some more meat on you." He nodded toward the other man in the room, "Dando, go and bring the kid a burger and a cream soda." Here he turned to me, "Or would you prefer a pastrami on rye?"

"A hamburger and soda is fine," I said. "Dando" was apparently Frank 'Dasher' Abbandando. He nodded and left. If the task disturbed him, he gave no sign of it. Maybe that's why he earned the nickname 'Dasher'. I couldn't help wondering if the seller would give the hamburger and soda to "Dando" free of charge out of fear, or if 'Dando' for the sake of his Sicilian sense of honor would insist on paying. And if so, would he ask Uncle Lepke to pay him back?

Uncle Lepke took me into an adjoining room and said I could rest on the sofa if I wanted to, and left. I was too excited to rest. Maybe there is a body under the sofa, I thought, not really, but maybe. No body. Nothing but a desk in the corner – a desk without a chair. That mystified me, but looking back, I guess he had a bigger desk somewhere else. I was disappointed that he hadn't asked my name.

'Dando' entered with the hamburger and cream soda and put them next to me on the sofa where I sat, not daring to rest. All I could think of was wait till the kids hear about my caper, if they would believe me. I wondered if there was something I could take with me as a souvenir of my visit. Maybe I could use it as a bribe to protect me from Flanagan, or to scare him off by proving who my uncle was, but of course I didn't dare to take anything, and an empty cream soda bottle proved nothing. And if Flanagan didn't believe the whole story, I would only earn another blow for "making up a whopper."

"Happy eating," 'Dando' said, and departed. A few minutes later he came back with a bunch of magazines. "Happy reading," he said. Comic books! My mother forbade me bringing comic books into the house. I read them on the sly at friends or anywhere outside I could find a spot to hide myself. She wouldn't be surprised at the gangsters having comic books, attributing their becoming gangsters to their having read comic books as youngsters. But the gangsters were grownups, not children. Apparently they still liked to read them. Did they get inspiration for their capers from them? I would like to have asked Uncle Lepke or 'Dando', but of course I did not.

Nor did I have the answer to another question which, so many years after my visit, pursues me. They say Buchalter and his 'Murder, Inc.' gang were responsible for 75 murders. (For one of which he subsequently died in the electric chair. "Good riddance," my mother said on hearing the news, but I felt sick to my stomach.) Did his mitzvah to me offset them in any way? There is a hasidic tale about a man brought before judgment in the next world. The angels shook their heads at his sins and were about to confine him to Sheol when one, looking over his life, pointed out that he had once helped a wagoner push his wagon out of the mud. The angels weighed on the scales of judgment the mud on the wheels against his sins and saw that they balanced. He was spared being sent to Sheol. But my meal, comic books, and afternoon sanctuary – what were they against 75 murders, or even one murder?

I doubted I contributed much to Buchalter's avoiding the severe decree.

The Wisdom of Solomon

ONE DAY, THE QUEEN OF SHEBA ARRIVED, determined to test the wisdom of King Solomon.

'Nu, Solomon," she asked. "Why did the peacock cross the road?"

Solomon immediately knew he was being tested.

"Hmm," he pondered on the answer. "Because the food was over there. Or maybe there were some female peacocks – perhaps wives or concubines. Or maybe there were some male peacocks and a pecking-order contest was soon to ensue."

He squinted at Sheba, who stood watching him, a smug expression on her beautiful face. No, he reasoned, it will take more than viable options to (1) remove that smug expression and (2) make her mine. Even the latter, I could forgo, but a political union with Sheba would be good geopolitics.

"Why did the peacock indeed cross the road?" he repeated rhetorically, in order to contemplate the question a bit more.

The queen of Sheba tapped her little ebony foot with impatience.

The gesture did not go unnoticed.

And then, as so often in the past, the solution suddenly materialized.

"To get to the other side," Solomon said.

"What?" said the Queen, who had been gazing with appreciation at Solomon's features, handsome in a rugged way.

Solomon repeated his solution to the riddle.

"The very solution!" exclaimed the Queen, amazed. She had formulated the riddle herself, including the answer. 'Why, you must be a mind-reader?"

"No, my queen, for us, sorcery is prohibited. But, of course, many other things are permitted."

Passage

Passage

IN THE YEAR 5779 since the creation, according to the Hebrew calendar, Rabbi Kolman, or the Heavenly Seer, as he was known to us, his disciples, was approaching the end of his days. Some said he was called the Heavenly Seer because of his holiness and his wisdom concerning the workings of Heaven; others, because of his interest in astronomy. His knowledge of the phenomena that made up the heavens – the Creation, he called it, or sometimes, the All – was vast; and his lectures were full of galaxies, planetary systems, nebulae, of which his disciples knew of as much as many astronomers, since the Seer spoke of them so much.

But of late, the Seer's lectures were becoming incoherent, like a dying star, flashes of brilliance followed by a longer subsiding, mumbling when his mind seemed to be elsewhere. Images and associations to white fire and black fire of Torah and galaxies and black spheres intermingled. We were afraid to exchange knowing glances and unknowing glances, but his deterioration and the confusing atmosphere was felt by all of us.

For a time, the Seer gave no sign he was aware of the changes in himself or of those they caused in us. The lighting of the sabbath candles, the prayers, the meditations continued at their appointed hours. One Friday night on the eve of the sabbath, after his lecture, again with the disconnectedness that had been increasing, he stopped in the middle and said something that convinced us he was mad. "Many times I have spoken of the stars, even to the furthest of the universe, and we have traveled there in thought together. And we have glimpsed Him, but only glimpsed. I want more than a glimpse; I want to travel to Him. To hasten the coming of the Messiah. My journey is repeated in the Torah, whenever your read it, you make the journey with me. Persevere."

The table was surrounded with a puzzled, embarrassed silence. Everyone waiting for him to continue speaking, prepared to discuss what we had heard, if indeed we had heard right. But the Seer did not continue. He persisted in his line of thought. A few followers dared to exchange fearful glances, fearful because they thought he may have crossed the border of sanity. He caught their looks but did not chastise them. "We have searched for Him together; I all my life. But it has not been enough, we have not found Him. He has been inaccessible, inaccessible. I want to tell Him it is time -- time to get closer to Him, to approach Him, to reach Him.

The Seer saw our puzzled looks. A new way of meditation, our eyes asked. He shook his head. "No, I am going to travel to Him, myself, in a chariot."

We were silent, interpreting what he said as a metaphor for his death. His eyes formed a smile, and his head shook. "Ah, yes, that too, but on the way, a journey, as I promised you, to the Source. I have taken our funds – the ones for the new building, and purchased a space ship."

Now we understood. The Seer quieted the hubbub before it could begin. "The building you would only name after me. We don't need a new building, we need to find The Builder of all things. You will go with me. Not your bodies, of course, but your minds, as when we would meditate together and our thoughts would be one. Your ascent to the higher worlds and to the borders of nothingness involves no motion on your part, for 'where you stand, there stands the All .'"

The logistics were simpler than we thought, the only limit being the psyche of the travelers. The mind could not stand the stress of long voyages. Six months was the longest. Beyond that, the mind could not stand the strain of separation. It was called simply, the Barrier.

The Barrier did not trouble the Seer; he wasn't bound to earth. "Our days upon earth are a shadow," he would say. He was searching for Him. "To end our exile. To bring about our redemption." The further he would travel from Earth meant the closer he would come to Him.

The days before departure were spent by the Seer and us in prayer. The Seer lectured only infrequently, and without power; we paid him a trifle less attention (that, under ordinary circumstances would be the same as turning our backs), but the thoughts of his court, his hasids, were on the journey ahead. If the Seer was going to physically travel to Him, our less direct methods seemed less important.

Finally, the day arrived, or rather the end of the day, for the Seer left at twilight when He is more accessible to the prayers of men. Like Elijah, the Seer headed for heaven in a chariot of flame, the prayer shawls of his disciples swaying in the fire's wind and the noise momentarily drowning our prayers.

In the weeks that followed, the Seer's flock attuned our minds to his, but heard nothing. We waited patiently; when the Seer was ready to share what he saw, he would contact us. And the beginnings of heaven were still far off. When six months passed, we worried about the Seer's approaching the Barrier, but when we heard nothing from him, we were relieved. If he lost his mind, we would know it instantly. And we reasoned that the Barrier separated man from himself, not from Him.

On a Friday night, almost a year after the Seer had departed, his thought reached us at the time set aside for meditation with him, following the evening service. We were not surprised, for we knew he would contract us. A few, younger, more headstrong, more doubting, feared he was deceased. It was to these doubting few, that his first words were addressed . I use "words" and not "thoughts", for it was more as if he was speaking to them "Those of you who thought I had returned to dust are mistaken. Do not rush me to that end before I complete my other journey."

Some rabbis said that what the Seer had said were the ramblings of a senile mind. In the years that passed, others said that the Seer never made the journey but remained in a room and communicated what he saw from there. Yet the Seer would have replied, "It isn't important in what form the journey is made."

Middle-School Golem

He was small, the child was, and not very handsome. And worse for him, gentle. An easy target for school bullies and their followers. And he was Jewish. There weren't any other Jewish kids in the school. He received taunts and sometimes beatings. Leo took it all, and hoped for an improvement, but no improvement came. Easter was the worst period, since the story of Jesus' crucifixion did not put the Jews in a good light. There were no Romans in the school on which to deflect responsibility.

Bruised in soul and body, he prayed for help. For a strong, tough Jewish boy to enter the school and mete out justice. For his parents to move. For the authorities, who did nothing, to act. For an earthquake to destroy the school.

But no help came.

One day, after school, seeking refuge in the library, he chanced upon a book. Someone had donated it many years before. It told the story of Rabbi Loew and his creation, the golem, who came to help defend the Jews of Prague against their enemies. The golem had been created from clay taken from near the river.

The next day after school Leo went to a creek (because the nearest river was too far away) and looking around to be sure no one could see him, took some mud from the bank. Unknown to him, he had been followed by the usual boys who wanted to have some "fun" with him. They were delighted when he went to the creek, since it offered all sorts of possibilities. They hid behind some bushes and waited to see what he would do.

"He is playing with mud," whispered one boy.

"A mud bath is a great idea."

Leo seemed to be building a castle. But it was too long, as one of the watching boys pointed out, seeing Leo's lengthened mound of clay. "When he finishes, we can bury him in it up to his neck." They watched, expectant.

Soon they discovered it was a figure. "Who's the person?" one whispered. "Maybe King David," they smirked, trying hard to figure what Leo was doing .

He seemed to be blowing upon the figure and saying something they couldn't hear. Leo looked to the sky, did something to the figure's forehead, and put his mouth close to the form's face once more.

One of the boys cried out, "I think it moved." The others shushed him, but they, too, had seen something strange.

Leo jumped back. Something had happened to the figure. For a moment, he thought it was the mud settling, but the movement was not like settling, rather the opposite. A shiver went through him that matched the shiver of his adversaries. Then a muddy arm reached up, while the second arm steadied the creature as it sat up.

Leo fell back onto the ground. The boys, further off, hiding behind the bushes, drew back, too.

The golem stood up, turned awkwardly toward Leo, who quickly got to his feet. He knew he was responsible for it.

The golem was his height, but stockier, and seemed even to grow slightly as he staggered toward his maker and made an awkward bow before him. Leo thought of the sheaves in Pharaoh's dream. Leo opened his mouth to say something, but the golem, already steadier of foot, walked past him, toward the bushes, crushing them underfoot, as the boys watched, horror stricken, frozen to the spot. He picked up one boy in each hand, as if they were cloth dolls. The third boy, terrified, ran.

Leo was afraid, too, but for a different reason -- he feared the golem would kill them. He wanted revenge, but choking them, or dashing them to death was going too far.

The golem held the two almost fainting boys and turned to face his master. He held them, waiting.

What was he waiting for? Leo wondered. And then he realized – for his command. The boys had turned white, their breathing was difficult, less from the tight grip of the golem than from terror.

Leo thought they had been punished enough. At the same time, he berated himself for being too good. Anyone else in his place would command the golem to knock their heads together. But Leo feared the golem might accidently kill them.

"Put them down," he commanded, unsure if the creature would obey.

The golem still held the boys, whose faces registered every degree between fear and wonderment because they heard the order and saw the result. Leo had control over the thing.

"Let go of them," Leo ordered.

The golem released them. They fell to the ground and both sat looking from Leo to the golem. It was difficult to know which they feared more.

"Get out of here," Leo ordered them.

They got to their feet and ran without looking back.

The golem stood before Leo, awaiting instructions.

Leo looked at the golem. He began to cry. Not from triumph, or relief, or vindication. From fear. He didn't know what to do with the golem. At first, he thought he would take him to school and wreak vengeance on the rest of his tormentors. But he knew in his heart he was incapable of that. And the authorities might throw him out of school. And if they feared to do it, his marks would suffer. It was impossible to study and be responsible for a golem – even a minor-golem. It just wouldn't work to pass off the golem as a new student.

Leo knew that, like Rabbi Loew, he would have to destroy the golem. And maybe that is why he cried, too. Because he had no friends in school, and even the golem would be better than nothing. But this creature was too much for him to handle. He wasn't a grownup, he couldn't keep the golem around longer, as did Rabbi Loew.

He asked the golem to forgive him, gave him a

hug, and erased the first of the Hebrew letters he had written with his finger on the golem's forehead. The golem fell face forward into the creek and dissolved slowly before Leo's eyes.

Yet the brief existence of the mini-golem had been sufficient. The three boys at first tried to tell the other school children what they had seen. Of course, no one believed them. Rather than continue to lose face (even blows were useless to convince the other kids of something like this), the three boys admitted it had all been a joke. But they stayed away from Leo, and prevented the other kids from bothering him. And if anyone dared to answer, "But he's Jewish …," they said, "So was Samson," and something in their faces dared anyone to say different.

Fomite

About Fomite

A fomite is a medium capable of transmitting infectious organisms from one individual to another.

"The activity of art is based on the capacity of people to be infected by the feelings of others." Tolstoy, *What Is Art?*

Writing a review on Amazon, Good Reads, Shelfari, Library Thing or other social media sites for readers will help the progress of independent publishing. To submit a review, go to the book page on any of the sites and follow the links for reviews. Books from independent presses rely on reader to reader communications.

For more information or to order any of our books, visit http://www.fomitepress.com/

More Titles from Fomite...

Novels
Joshua Amses — *During This, Our Nadir*
Joshua Amses — *Ghatsr*
Joshua Amses — *Raven or Crow*
Joshua Amses — *The Moment Before an Injury*
Jaysinh Birjepatel — *Nothing Beside Remains*
Jaysinh Birjepatel — *The Good Muslim of Jackson Heights*
David Brizer — *Victor Rand*
Paula Closson Buck — *Summer on the Cold War Planet*
Dan Chodorkoff — *Loisaida*
David Adams Cleveland — *Time's Betrayal*
Jaimee Wriston Colbert — *Vanishing Acts*
Roger Coleman — *Skywreck Afternoons*
Marc Estrin — *Hyde*
Marc Estrin — *Kafka's Roach*
Marc Estrin — *Speckled Vanities*
Zdravka Evtimova — *In the Town of Joy and Peace*
Zdravka Evtimova — *Sinfonia Bulgarica*
Daniel Forbes — *Derail This Train Wreck*
Greg Guma — *Dons of Time*
Richard Hawley — *The Three Lives of Jonathan Force*
Lamar Herrin — *Father Figure*
Michael Horner — *Damage Control*
Ron Jacobs — *All the Sinners Saints*

Fomite

Ron Jacobs — *Short Order Frame Up*
Ron Jacobs — *The Co-conspirator's Tale*
Scott Archer Jones — *And Throw Away the Skins*
Scott Archer Jones — *A Rising Tide of People Swept Away*
Julie Justicz — *Degrees of Difficulty*
Maggie Kast — *A Free Unsullied Land*
Darrell Kastin — *Shadowboxing with Bukowski*
Coleen Kearon — *#triggerwarning*
Coleen Kearon — *Feminist on Fire*
Jan English Leary — *Thicker Than Blood*
Diane Lefer — *Confessions of a Carnivore*
Rob Lenihan — *Born Speaking Lies*
Douglas Milliken — *Our Shadow's Voice*
Colin Mitchell — *Roadman*
Ilan Mochari — *Zinsky the Obscure*
Peter Nash — *Parsimony*
Peter Nash — *The Perfection of Things*
George Ovitt — Stillpoint
George Ovitt — Tribunal
Gregory Papadoyiannis — *The Baby Jazz*
Pelham — *The Walking Poor*
Andy Potok — *My Father's Keeper*
Frederick Ramey — *Comes A Time*
Joseph Rathgeber — *Mixedbloods*
Kathryn Roberts — *Companion Plants*
Robert Rosenberg — *Isles of the Blind*
Fred Russell — *Rafi's World*
Ron Savage — *Voyeur in Tangier*
David Schein — *The Adoption*
Lynn Sloan — *Principles of Navigation*
L.E. Smith — *The Consequence of Gesture*
L.E. Smith — *Travers' Inferno*
L.E. Smith — *Untimely RIPped*
Bob Sommer — *A Great Fullness*
Tom Walker — *A Day in the Life*
Susan V. Weiss — *My God, What Have We Done?*
Peter M. Wheelwright — *As It Is On Earth*
Suzie Wizowaty — *The Return of Jason Green*

Poetry
Anna Blackmer — *Hexagrams*
Antonello Borra — *Alfabestiario*
Antonello Borra — *AlphaBetaBestiaro*

Fomite

Fomite

Susan Thomas — *The Empty Notebook Interrogates Itself*
Paolo Valesio/Todd Portnowitz — *La Mezzanotte di Spoleto/ Midnight in Spoleto*
Sharon Webster — *Everyone Lives Here*
Tony Whedon — *The Tres Riches Heures*
Tony Whedon — *The Falkland Quartet*
Claire Zoghb — *Dispatches from Everest*

Stories
Jay Boyer — *Flight*
L. M Brown — *Treading the Uneven Road*
Michael Cocchiarale — *Here Is Ware*
Michael Cocchiarale — *Still Time*
Neil Connelly — *In the Wake of Our Vows*
Catherine Zobal Dent — *Unfinished Stories of Girls*
Zdravka Evtimova —*Carts and Other Stories*
John Michael Flynn — *Off to the Next Wherever*
Derek Furr — *Semitones*
Derek Furr — *Suite for Three Voices*
Elizabeth Genovise — *Where There Are Two or More*
Andrei Guriuanu — *Body of Work*
Zeke Jarvis — *In A Family Way*
Arya Jenkins — *Blue Songs in an Open Key*
Jan English Leary — *Skating on the Vertical*
Marjorie Maddox — *What She Was Saying*
William Marquess — *Boom-shacka-lacka*
Gary Miller — *Museum of the Americas*
Jennifer Anne Moses — *Visiting Hours*
Martin Ott — *Interrogations*
Christopher Peterson — *Amoebic Simulacra*
Jack Pulaski — *Love's Labours*
Charles Rafferty — *Saturday Night at Magellan's*
Ron Savage — *What We Do For Love*
Fred Skolnik— *Americans and Other Stories*
Lynn Sloan — *This Far Is Not Far Enough*
L.E. Smith — *Views Cost Extra*
Caitlin Hamilton Summie — *To Lay To Rest Our Ghosts*
Susan Thomas — *Among Angelic Orders*
Tom Walker — *Signed Confessions*
Silas Dent Zobal — *The Inconvenience of the Wings*

Odd Birds
William Benton — *Eye Contact: Writing on Art*

Fomite

Micheal Breiner — *the way none of this happened*
J. C. Ellefson — *Under the Influence: Shouting Out to Walt*
David Ross Gunn — *Cautionary Chronicles*
Andrei Guriuanu and Teknari — *The Darkest City*
Gail Holst-Warhaft — *The Fall of Athens*
Roger Lebovitz — *A Guide to the Western Slopes and the Outlying Area*
Roger Lebovitz — *Twenty-two Instructions for Near Survival*
dug Nap— *Artsy Fartsy*
Delia Bell Robinson — *A Shirtwaist Story*
Peter Schumann — *Belligerent & Not So Belligerent Slogans from the Possibilitarian Arsenal*
Peter Schumann — *Bread & Sentences*
Peter Schumann — *Charlotte Salomon*
Peter Schumann — *Faust 3*
Peter Schumann — *Planet Kasper, Volumes One and Two*
Peter Schumann — *We*

Plays
Stephen Goldberg — *Screwed and Other Plays*
Michele Markarian — *Unborn Children of America*

Essays
Robert Sommer — *Losing Francis: Essays on the Wars at Home*